CRAZY LOVE

ELIAS MIGUEL MUÑOZ

ARTE PUBLICO PRESS

This volume is made possible by a grant from the National Endowment for the Arts, a federal agency, and the Texas Commission for the Arts.

Arte Publico Press
University of Houston
Houston, Texas 77004

Muñoz, Elías Miguel
Crazy Love.
   I. Title.
PS3563.U494C7   1988   863   88-6394
ISBN 0-934770-83-2

THIS BOOK

This book could not have been written without the support of several people. I would like to express my debt of gratitude to Karen Christian, who proofread and edited the text, offering insightful comments. I am also indebted to Curtis Smith, who shared with me his passion for music. I thank Karen Calloway for sparking in me the idea of writing something in English. And Bill Artz for being my first reader and literary critic.

The two writers whose friendship and work had the most to do with this book are Nicholasa Mohr and Rolando Hinojosa. I thank them for the experiences they shared with me one November day, and for keeping in touch ever since.

I thank my friends at Arte Público and *The Americas Review*, Nicolás Kanellos, Marina Tristán, Julian Olivares, for making this and many other publications possible. And Harry Caicedo from *Vista Magazine*, for a memorable comida cubana and the dialogue he provided on the subject of widening the audience.

I would like to thank, last but certainly not least, my sister Virginia, for her love and her poems.

E. M. M.

To Mari Nelle Rogers, a dear friend,
for understanding.

"At the hour of his death, if there is time and lucidity,
Lucas will ask to hear two things: Mozart's last quintet and
a certain piano solo on the theme of 'I Ain't Got No Body.'
If he feels there won't be enough time, he'll only ask for
the piano record. Long is the list, but he's already
chosen . . ."

(Julio Cortázar, *A Certain Lucas*, translated from the
Spanish by Gregory Rabassa)

"I love you so
but I still know
it's a crazy love . . ."

(Paul Anka, "Crazy Love," from the 1963 RCA
recording *Paul Anka's 21 Golden Hits*)

STEPS

STEP ONE

This Evil World

I have seen love between you and Abuelo. He will slowly raise his hand and touch your hair, your forehead, your eyes, your shoulders. He will smile faintly, murmuring something about how fat Eusebia's sister is, the Gordita. Then Abuela will rush onto the scene and try to make him see reality: "That's not my sister, Raúl. That's your granddaughter, Genny!" His smile quickly fades. He clenches his fists and starts hitting anything within reach. Then Abuela turns to me and sobs, "You know, Nito, I'm scared. He's calling his brothers who have been dead for years. His father, for Heaven's sake! He calls for his father. And he thinks Geneia is my little sister. I won't stand for that, because my sister died when she was fifteen. I won't stand for such confusion. He needs to know that that's his granddaughter!"

Mami's fifty. Hard to believe. She looks much younger. Mami and I became good friends when I was ten or eleven, during an "operation." She had just bought some powerful spray to kill roaches. And it worked! The insects came running out, desperately running away from the poison. Many got through the door and into the back yard. What a feast that must've been for the chickens. They flocked and devoured the dying roaches within a few seconds. Mami started crying, "The chickens, Julianito, the chickens! They'll die, and your father will kill me!" So I suggested that we cut open their bellies and take out the poisoned roaches and sew them up again and then take care of them with bread, milk and love. Mami brought out a couple of needles, a Gillette razor, some thread. We cleaned everything with alcohol, gathered up the chickens, took them into the kitchen, and played surgeon. We lost four of the nine birds. We thought that maybe those were the ones who had eaten the most. But we saved the rest. We built a home for them next to the house. Papi never found out.

Lately Mami has begun to talk about the past. "What's gotten into her?" asks Abuela. "She used to be such a docile creature, never raised her voice, never talked back to me, always listened and took my advice." It's all because of this damned country, she says. This evil world has turned her darling daughter into a monster. Because Mami won't call her ten times a day, and she won't consult with her when a major decision has to be made, and she won't allow her to put ideas about femininity and little-girl-duties into your head. Because she fights her, and hangs up on her when Abuela starts telling her what to do. We can't change what happened before you came, Geneia. But we can do a lot to make your future different. Mami says that you will be free. You won't be fearful, quiet. You're a tomboy, according to Abuela. "Geneia doesn't sit and smile when we have company, she doesn't call me to ask about my health, she doesn't run to me the way Nito and Johnny used to run, to kiss me and hug me. Geneia doesn't love me the way the boys did." Abuela's right, of course. I haven't seen love between you and her.

Mami says that Abuela got married at an even younger age than she did. She was a strong young woman, so Abuelo married her and took her with him to his father's farm, where all his brothers lived, and made her their servant. None of his nine brothers was married, and there were no women in the family. Abuelo's mother had recently died. The house was a shambles. So Abuela was heaven sent. The campesinos left at five-thirty in the morning to go work in the fields. By the time they were ready to eat, a sumptuous breakfast had to be waiting on the table. During the day the young wife also had to feed the animals, cut the wood, get the water from the well, tend to the house, hand wash and iron all the clothes, and prepare all the other meals. On Sundays they would kill and roast a pig, which was served with buckets of greasy white rice, black beans, fried ripe plantain, and boiled yuca. Abuela cooked for her "men" and served them the entire day.

Husband and wife moved to the neighborhood Zonalegre in Santa Clara after a few years. By now our grandmother had a hernia from the excessive work. And she was pregnant. Mami's birth did her a great deal of damage. Abuela's organs never returned to their normal positions. She started to wear a girdle and got fat, really fat. The skin between her breasts and her stomach was always raw; the cracks would burst and would be very painful. Then Abuela would strip to the waist and lie flat on the floor, looking up at the guano ceiling, and she would air her wounds with a homemade fan. Her hernia began to show through the girdle. I remember the tight green dress she used to wear and her white skirt with flowers painted all over it, her strutting, bulging silhouette in the bright sunshine, her legs curved from the tremendous weight, her pace, fast and determined.

My Big Bro Nito has curly hair. My Big Bro Nito
has a pretty beard and mustach that I love.
And most of all I love Big Bro Nito cos he loves
me . . .

byby love Geni

A Precious Gift

Johnny tells me that Abuelo has been dead for a long time. That's not Tabaquito sitting there like a vegetable, he says. Our grandfather is gone. Johnny remembers the long walks he used to take with our grandfather along the beach, in Varadero first and later in Redondo, and the times they'd get up at dawn and go fishing. They'd come back with half a dozen stinking fish, and our grandpa would be so proud. Johnny remembers the hours Abuelo used to put in for him, in Gardena, collecting bottles that would eventually be traded in for money at the store. That's not his Tabaquito sitting there like a vegetable, he says.

Abuela jokes about the fact that Abuelo's cleaner now than he has ever been. After his stroke he decided he hated water, she says, so he went for about two months without taking a shower. "Can you imagine? I had to sleep with him!" I remember Abuelo as a short and temperamental man. He liked to complain about everything. He argued with Abuela. I used to think that that was the only way he could express himself, talking loud and angrily. But there were times when he became the most tender of men. He lifted me up and sat me on his lap and asked me just one question, "How are you, Julián?" Abuelo worked in the sugar cane fields. He would come home when it was dark, eat supper, and sit on the porch with a Havana cigar, his tabaquito that burned away all evening, while he told stories of apparitions and teased the young girls who gathered around to listen and visit with me.

Abuela would take a bus to come see us on the affluent side of town every day of the week. She had dreams of having a big house and of taking me there to live with her. She would buy me a big television set and lots of colored pencils. She would invite all my pretty girlfriends and she would dress me up real nice in an embroidered shirt, a guayabera. She would comb my hair with the best grease that she could find in Bolita's kiosk, and she would drench me with cologne. Prince charming, *her* prince charming, dressed to kill.

Zonalegre was noisy with the voices of merchants selling tamales and sugar cane drinks. And there was always a bolero or an American song playing on the jukebox at the kiosk. Abuela loved Paul Anka's songs, "Diana," "Put your head on my shoulder." "Adam and Eve." Whenever they played "Crazy Love," she would take me in her arms, an ocean of garlic and cilantro, and start moving her hips. She was a powerful body that held me and danced with crazy love.

Next door to Grandma lived Amelia's family. Six, seven people were crammed into a small box made of wood, zinc and cardboard. Amelia was cross-eyed and spoke in drawn-out sentences. She had quite a temper. Things had to be done this way or that way. Her way. There were two boys in the family, Octavio and Eufemio. They were dark and skinny. We weren't friends. They liked to tease me and call me mariquita. Once they stood in front of me, both stark naked in the middle of the room, and started playing with themselves. Amelia also had three girls. Zenia, Matilde and Mayda. I loved their names. I couldn't understand how anyone could think of such mysterious names. Happiness, claimed Father, was something that only the rich, or the almost-rich like us could know. Yet no one I knew seemed happier than Amelia's girls. We'd play house together. We had to hide from Grandma when we did that, because boys were not supposed to play house. I was always the head of the family, of course, or the chauffeur, or the son. I would go hunting for lizard eggs in the outhouse; the girls would fry them and pretend to eat them. Grandma told us stories about little boys and girls who died from eating those tiny lizard eggs. They were poisonous, and we were supposed to keep away from them.

One day I was sitting on our porch when Zenia, Amelia's oldest daughter, got home. I figured Zenia must've done something wrong, because as soon as she walked in the door, Amelia came out from behind it, holding a large piece of wood in her hands, and hit Zenia on her back, on her legs, on her hips.

Abuela's eyes shine when she remembers the beatings she used to give me. I turn to you, Geneia, and wonder what you're thinking. You haven't known physical pain. You have never experienced a slap, a kick, a fist in your face or your stomach. You're a lucky girl who knows only psychological torture: long silences, violent screaming and prohibitions.

Abuela insists on reminding me that she raised me. My mother was young, much too young, she says, and didn't know how to bring up a little boy properly. How could Mami show me the important things in life when she was still playing with dolls? Papi was a salesman, always on the go, and he would take Mami along on his trips sometimes. So Abuela took charge of the first-born from the very beginning. She bathed me, she fed me. Later she would decide what clothes I was to wear, what shoes, the way I should act, the words I should use. Papi hated her for it. He still hates her. "Your grandma's showing you her stupid hick ways again, behind my back!," he used to say. "Backward campesino mentality!"

Grandma turns to me, smiling, and says, "Remember

when you misbehaved and I took out your grandfather's belt and hit you, and I made your butt bleed, and you cried? Remember? I was the one who taught you to know good from bad." She tried, anyway. I was awakened by her and her brother Marcos one morning. They were whispering and staring at me. "What a hunk of a boy, don't you think? What a little machito." Marcos came close, sat on the edge of the bed, took my tiny member in his hands, and explained that God had given me this precious gift, that I should always guard it, and never use it to hurt girls. He said some day I would find a good woman and this thingy would bring us both lots of happiness and joy.

One morning, Geneia, I woke up and found a piece of paper in the sheets. I looked at it and felt frightened. I ran and showed it to her. "What is this, Abuela? Why was it in my bed? Who are all those people? Why are they being burned?" And she proceeded to tell me about Heaven and Earth, demons and angels, punishment for sins and the lesson to be learned: "I don't know how that paper got there. It was probably an angel, your guardian angel, looking out for you, so you remember to always be good, so that you don't end up in Hell like those poor souls, so that one day, when you die, God will take you up to Heaven with Him and his Saints."

April fool's day!!

Dear brother Nito I really miss you a lot. Really I do every night and not even only at night but every minute and second of my heart's beat I miss you. I am writing this little letter because I want to send you this little picture of me and you together. Remember at the party we took a picture? Well I am going to send you that one. But Mom wants to send it to. So its from both of us.

LOVE   Geneia

Abuela's Secret

Father said that Grandma lived on the poor side of town, that he hated to see me go there and mingle with all that good-for-nothing scum. Mother argued with him about that. He had no right, she would say, to criticize her parents for being poor. No one wanted to be poor. They had no choice about the way they lived and they weren't common criminals to be insulted like that.

Father never listened. He raised hell every time I asked to spend the weekend in Zonalegre with my grandma. He took me there reluctantly and cursed the whole way. I never spoke when he acted upset. I feared his strength and his anger. One simple blow of his hand could destroy me (I knew this much too well). I dreaded the trip and reveled in my grandmother's welcoming arms. She always had a treat, a milk dessert, bananas, mamey, guava paste, sweetened ice cubes. Father would say a few words, something about using a fork, napkins, washing my hands before and after meals, brushing my teeth regularly. Grandma listened quietly, obediently. Anything, whatever he wanted was fine, as long as he would let me stay with her a few days, even a few hours.

I had friends on the poor side of town. They always gathered around me when I arrived, and looked at my clothes, and caressed my hair. They would run after our car for a block, waving and welcoming me. Actually, not all the kids in Zonalegre were my friends . . . *Bolita's Kiosk, the smell of fried pork and plantain, the music of the jukebox, Crazy Love, You are my crazy love, the arm that chokes me, the hands that hold my arms behind my back, that press down on my mouth and seal it, the harsh voices of children. It's dark. They push me. I fall on the floor; they hold me down hard; they pull down my pants, I try to lift my head. Among them I see Amelia's boys. They're waiting their turn . . .*

Grandma was alarmed when she saw me. She cried until Grandpa came home. She made me promise not to tell him anything. This was going to be our secret. She cleaned me up, put iodine on my scratches, which I was to say were caused by a fall, and she had me sit in warm water for some time. It would heal, she said, and no one would ever be able to tell. "Tell what?," I asked her. She didn't answer. She just told me to trust her.

Dear Brother Nito

I'm real better now but my right ear is real badly stuffed up, doctor said it's nothing to worry about He said I could do everything I want even go swimming! Thats fantastic Huh?

Hey. Mommy won 2 tickets to go see Shark 3D want to go see it? Mom doesn't want to go see it for two reasons 1st she's scared of going alone with me 2nd she doesn't want to see 3D because its too much like real life for her.

You know Papi is going to buy me a dog. I'm going to name her PRINCESS. I'll name her that because every one can say it easy. I hope you come soon. I'm going to keep on taking care of myself. Remember I love you the size of the universe!

Luv ya

Geneia

What It Takes

Grandma was very protective of her only daughter. It was a dangerous world out there and she wasn't going to let it ruin her baby. So she locked her up and didn't let her go to school. Years later, after the Revolution, my mom took classes and got a high school diploma. She was bitterly criticized by her mother. How could a decent woman lower herself and go to school with all those communists? A woman's place was in her home with her children, not in books. Grandma hates Castro. But Father says that she adored him in the beginning. She would cut his picture out of the newspaper and paste it on the wall. Once she dressed me up as a Miliciano and had me pose for a series of photo portraits. He was Christ for her, the Messiah. I still don't understand how he could have possibly let her down so badly, how it could've possibly been better for her under Batista.

Mother says that Father used to come around in a big car and sing to her. One day he asked for her hand, so she packed her things and went off to Havana to get married and go on a honeymoon. Mother was never asked if she loved him. He was handsome, strong, had a good Spanish name and a Cadillac convertible. What more could she want? She couldn't turn down the chance to leave Zonalegre, to have a better life.

My first memories of them as a young couple are enticing. They kissed a lot. And they were noisy at night when they made love. You could tell when they got it on. Mother had a neck full of hickies the next morning. Father spent time at home in those days and courted her. In the evening we would go to the park or a movie, or we would ride in a horse carriage along Calle Independencia. When Father was away on business for a long time, they had passionate sexual encounters upon his return. Johnny and I would stay in the living room, pretending to watch a movie on TV, and we would listen to them and beat off quietly. Sometimes, when we were really excited, we masturbated each other.

Father had a huge penis that he liked to flaunt every chance he got. We were under the terrible impression that he made Mother bleed. She had the habit of leaving her panties in a bundle on the edge of the bathtub, and the blood was there, clearly visible. On weekends, when Father was still in bed, he would call us kids and show us his erection. "This is what it takes to be a man," he would say. He tried to fuck me once, in his sleep, not realizing that it wasn't his wife that was lying next to him. I used to fear the dark and suffered from terrible nightmares. On those nights I was allowed to sleep with one of them. The night of the "accident," Mother left me her place next to Father and went to sleep in my bed. I was awakened by what I first thought was Father's leg or his arm, between my cheeks; but both his arms were holding my waist and his legs were wrapped around mine. It started to hurt and I made a move to break away. He woke up immediately and rolled over to his side of the bed, breathing heavily and pretending to be asleep.

It's hard to believe that Johnny was the one who told me, when he was only six, about "the period," "fucking," and "coming." He started to need sex at a very early age, so he got it in whatever way he could. Once in a while he'd fuck the chickens, but most of the time he just let Ruben, the little boy next door, suck him off. When Ruben left the country with his family, I told Johnny that if he wanted to, we could suck each other off, but he said no, that was a sin and we would probably be punished and lose our pricks if we did it.

As soon as I started showing signs of artistic behavior they took me to the doctor. They felt that a boy my age should not spend so much time writing songs and daydreaming. Johnny got to go too, maybe so the doctor could have a "normal" kid as a point of reference. The doctor didn't find anything wrong with me, but in order to satisfy my parents' anxiety, he prescribed a series of hormonal injections. My brother got them also. Johnny, according to the doctor, had overgrown testicles, a common occurrence in Caribbean children of very young parents. I had to have the shots not because I needed them, the doctor said, but only as a preventive measure. Hormonal fluid never hurt anybody, he claimed, and the shots might help me grow lots of hair and become a real Macho Cubano.

I had been masturbating regularly for quite some time now, with no major consequences. But oh, those shots were the cause of serious preoccupations. One night, during a passionate session, something came out of my picha. I was terrified. Was I being punished, like Johnny thought we would for playing with each other, being brothers and all? Or was that slimy stuff part of the medication that didn't want to stay in my body? I pretended nothing had happened and went at it again the next night. No luck, though. There was that crap coming out of me again, and again at the height of my pleasure. Up to now I'd had it easy. I would rub my thighs against each other anywhere, even in class, and the friction would bring about that feeling of relief, like a tickling that ran from my toes to my neck. The Math teacher had caught me in the act once. She asked me in front of the entire class, "Are you riding your bike over there, Julianito?"

I talked to Johnny about it. He simply said I was "coming" already, and was envious of me: He wasn't "coming" yet. "What am I supposed to do about it?," I asked. "Nothing," he answered, "just clean it off with a towel, and don't stick it in a girl." I was pissed. One evening, while Father was taking a shower, Mother asked me to go in and talk to him. "Go on. He wants to see you." My father stopped singing when he saw me and asked me to sit down on the toilet. I handed him a towel and he started to dry himself off. "How's your picha doing?" he asked. "Fine, still there," I replied. "And your pelotas?" "Fine too, thanks." He asked me to take my pants down and show him. I did. He was pleased to see the hair and the apparent growth of my organs. He told me there was some stuff in there that would start to come out any minute now, like milk, he said, and I wasn't to worry about it. Most of all, I wasn't to play with myself to make it come out. Beating off made people dumb. Boys who masturbate, he insisted, grow up to be faggots and idiots.

Dear Nito

Here's my Little Prince report. How you like it?

THE LITTLE PRINCE ALONE ON A LITTLE PLANET NO LARGER THAN A HOUSE. MY HOUSE! HE OWNED THREE VOLCANOS, TWO ACTIVE AND ONE ENXTINCT. HE OWNED A LITTLE FLOWER, NOT LIKE ANY OTHER FLOWER IN ALL SPACE OF GREAT BEAUTY WHEN HE SAW THAT FLOWER THE LITTLE PRINCE STARTED ON INTERPLANETERY TRAVELS THAT BROUGHT HIM TO EARTH WHERE HE LEARNED FINALLY FROM A FOX THE SECRET OF WHAT LIFE REALLY MEANS! AND ONE DAY WHEN HE WAS TRAVELING IN THE AFRICAN DESERT HE SAT DOWN WITH THE FOX IN THE EVENING WITH THE COOL BREEZE BLOWING HIS HAIR HE DISAP- PEARED JUST LIKE A SNAP! AND THE LITTLE FOX GOT UP AND WENT BACK TO HIS CAVE.

By-By Big Bro!

Little Princess,

Gennita

Be Quiet When I Talk

In the evenings, after supper, we would all sit outside, on the porch, and Papi would sing the songs that I heard in Bolita's kiosk, especially the boleros, he knew them all. Once in while Johnny and I would join in, if we knew the song. What a spectacular trio, the neighbors would say, Father and Sons, how wonderful, they're better than the Panchos.

Mami told me that a record producer from Havana had heard Papi once, when he was a little boy, and this man asked Abuelo Toledo if he would let his son go to the capital to get voice training and sign with a big company. But Toledo refused to let Papi go. Instead, he bought him a bike and told him that there was work to be done in life and singers didn't have it in them to bring home the bacon.

When I said that I wanted to take piano lessons Papi just laughed. "Piano lessons? Boys are not supposed to play the piano. Go outside and play baseball, muchacho." A few days later I said, at the table, that with or without piano lessons I was going to be a musician someday. He was very upset. How was I going to support a family with a musician's wages? Those people never had work and they had to be very famous, like Ñico Membiela, Bobby Cap" and Vicentico Valdés before they could make a decent living. He said that it was too soon for me to decide what I was going to be, anyway, that I had to study abroad first, in the great North, and some day I would probably be able to have my own business, a department store or a clothing factory.

Later, Papi informed us that we were all going to leave for the great North. That's when Abuela built a huge altar in one corner of her house, where she would kneel and pray to her saints. She'd put food and black coins in front of the pictures. In the center was the Virgen del Cobre, matron of the island. Around her were saints of all colors and forms: old, young, children, male, female, fat, skinny, with short hair, with long hair, without hair; they all had the same pained look and their eyes turned upward, like they had had enough. Sometimes Abuela invited Amelia and two other neighbors and they prayed together. Amelia sat in the middle, stuck her fingers in a cup of water and sprinkled the saints several times, like her fingers were burning. I sat outside when this happened. Abuela asked me to please sit there quietly and not to let anyone in, not even Abuelo.

The routine never changed: right before we left the house to go run an errand or visit a neighbor, she would look me in the eye, and warn me, "Now, Nito, we are going to be out there together. I want people to think you are a well behaved child, asentadito. You be quiet when I talk and obey me. Understand? Because if you don't, as much as I love you, when we get back home I'll have to give you a good spanking." She would take out one of Grandpa's belts and she'd lay it on the floor, by the door: "There it is, waiting if you misbehave." Sure enough, she meant every word of it.

The first time she hit me I thought I was going to die, not so much from the physical pain as from my disappointment in her. We were visiting one of the neighbors, a thin woman who had three children. Grandma told me to sit beside her and not to move. I really wanted to go to the backyard where the kids were playing. When she got excited about something she was saying I slipped away and went outside. She followed me, furious, and didn't say a word, just looked at me with her typical sinister eyes, grabbed me by the hand, and threw me in the chair. All the way home she kept talking about how I was going to get it, how she wasn't going to be disobeyed by me ever again. I don't remember if I talked back to her when she was beating me, or if I took it quietly. I do remember that for days afterwards I didn't want to see her.

The second time was even more painful, because it involved Amelia. Grandma found me and Mayda in the outhouse, playing at having sex. She scolded us and spoke quietly to us about God and sin and then Mayda got scared and ran back to her house. Amelia came over after a while. She didn't even say hi to Grandma, just walked straight to where I was sitting and pinched the inside of my thighs. Then she started yelling at me, "What did you do to my daughter, you little pig, rich piece of shit? If you want to get yourself a woman, you let me know next time, and I'll get you one, for money, but my daughter is sacred, you hear? Just because your father has a big car and twenty guayaberas doesn't mean that you are going to come around here and take advantage of us. You keep away from my little girl, you rich piece of shit!"

You can imagine what happened after Amelia left, can't you?

Dear Nito,

How are things over there? I'm doin fine. Well, just OK,
not that great. You know why? I'm having trouble in my
school. The teacher, Mrs. Morson, is mad at me. And they
called Papi the other day and he had to come and get me. And
he talked real hard to me but I didn't cry. And he said to me,
Genny, you can't behave like that, you're a nice girl. Why you
do that for? And Mami, Mami was sad when she found out.
    The problem? Well, I dont know how to explain it to
you, Big Bro. It's kinda hard. The reason Papi was mad at me
and Mrs. Morson called him and they almost suspended me
was that I bite (bit?) one of my classmates on the arm, real
hard. He was bugging me and taking my pencils and calling
me Perra, Genny the Perra. And then the other kids started
calling me Perra, Genny the Dog, too. Because they said that
I barked just like a dog. And I did! Just like Princess. And so
I got mad at this kid and I showed him how much of a perra I
could be. I bit him so hard and could taste his blood!
    Mrs. Morson told Papi that I need to see a doctor, one of
those children doctors for the head, when you're kinda
cuckoo, you know, a little loco. She says I need lotsa help,
because she says that I think Im a dog. I guess shes right,
Nito. Sometimes I act like Princess because I like her, and
she's my only friend and I spend a lot of time with her and
another thing, you will believe me, no Nito? another thing is
that, well, she talks to me, and I understand everything she
says. And she says that you have to defend yourself with your
teeth when people are mean to you, bite them, she says, and
show them how strong you are. And she says when their nice
you stick out your tongue and lick them, and give them lotsa
kisses that way, and that's what I do, Nito. I licked Grandma
the other day and she gave me that look, you know, the serious look, and was quiet. Grandma doesn't like Princess. She

says Princess is dangerious (sp?) like a lion. And I say great, let her be like a lion!

The other day Grandma came to visit and Princess put her two big paws all over her and she made her fall flat on the floor. And Mami came running and asking Abuela if she was alrite. Grandma says we have to get rid of that dog. She says the dog is bad for me. But you know Grandma, she raised you, no? She says she raised you. She complains all the time about the way I behave. She says I'm not asentadita, how do you say that in English, asentadita? Like, you know, real calm and ladylike and quiet. She says I don't behave like a normal little girl. And that's what Mrs. Morson told Papi, too. She told him that I didn't behave normal, like I should. What do you think, Nito?

Well, enouf of that, I'm getting tired of writin all this stuff. Next time you come I'll give you a million hugs and kisses.

Love ya!

Geneia the Perrita

The Altar Boy

I was a devout Catholic boy. I truly believed that that was Christ up there on the cross and that God could do miracles. I went to Mass twice a week, Sunday mornings and Wednesday nights with the old maids; I had taken communion, I had been confirmed, and I was a reliable Altar Boy. One Sunday, after Mass, Father Castellanos asked me to stay around to help him. There were some statues of saints in the basement that he wanted to bring up, and they were too heavy for one person alone. So I stayed. I helped him with two of the statues and as we went down for the third one, he took me by the arm, sort of like holding me. Then he touched my thighs and said they were big and strong for such a young boy. He asked me if I had other things that were big, like my toes or anything. I said I didn't know, and he smiled, sweat beading on his brow, and he said he bet he could find nice big things between my legs. So he unzipped my pants and grabbed my prick. Up close, he looked like we thought all Spaniards looked: black greasy hair, large bushy eyebrows, long eyelashes, thin lips, eyes that twinkled. He must've been a young priest.

I decided I didn't want to see Father Castellanos for a long time after he seduced me. So the next Saturday I told Mother that I wouldn't be going to church with her on Sunday. She thought I was joking. Such a religious boy, how could I refuse to go to Sunday Mass. I insisted, so she called Father and complained to him. He wasn't in the habit of going to church with any frequency; maybe for a baptism, or to accompany Mother when he had just bought her a new dress and she needed to show it off. Most of the time I went to church alone. But this time he would go, he said. The entire family would go.

Sunday morning I stayed in bed too long after Mother

called me. I was to hurry to make the nine o'clock Mass. I said no, I didn't want to go. You will go, she said, or I'll tell your father. Tell him, tell that son of a bitch, I yelled. Son of a bitch. He came out running, half naked, with a sheet wrapped around his waist. He couldn't believe his ears, he said. Had he really heard me say those words? I am not going to church, I repeated. Get up, right this minute, he ordered me. No, I replied. So he picked me up from the bed and threw me against the wall. I noticed then, when the sheet fell off, that he had a bandage around his penis. He pulled me by the hair towards the bed again, slapped me hard several times, and ordered me to say that I would go to church. No, I responded, no and no. So he started hitting my face with a closed fist. It felt like he was breaking it into little pieces. When Mami saw the blood she tried to pull him away from me, begging him to let go, to leave me alone, not to hit me anymore. He pushed her aside and went for my stomach. He hit it twice. By now I couldn't move. Every pore of my body ached.

The face I saw in the mirror, a few minutes later, was swollen and gray. It wasn't my face.

Dear Nito,

    How are things over there? Is it cold in New Jersey? I can't wait until I go over there. Papi said he will let me, if I go with Mami. He's such a good Daddy. You know, the idea of going on an airplane sounds pretty cool to me. I want a seat by the window of the plane so I could see the clouds and daydream. You know what I'm going to daydream about? Flash Gordon, you know, the part where the sun and the sky turned all red . . .

LOVE,

Whizzer Spinner

The Most Terrible Memory

Why? Why not the good memories? Like Reyes Magos, January sixth, when I couldn't sleep waiting for that glorious morning, when I would get up and run to the living room and find the walls, the floor, every corner covered with toys. "The Three Wise Men were here," Mother would tell me, "and they left messages for you. They said that if you keep behaving like a good little boy, they will continue to bring you toys each year. They seemed happy, Julianito. And look! Look at all those regalos!"

The last year we were in Cuba, a few days before Reyes Magos, Mother left the house early in the morning. They had received a supply of some medication at the corner pharmacy, she said, and she was going to stand in line for a few hours to try to get some of whatever they were selling. I followed her. She didn't go to the pharmacy. She went beyond it, to the store. I sat there, hiding, and waited for her from a distance. They opened the store, the crowd barged in, and some time later she came out, her arms full of boxes containing my presents and Johnny's. When she found me she looked sadder than I had ever seen her. "What are you doing here?" she asked. "Waiting for you, Mami, to help you with the toys." She seemed so disappointed. "You know, Julianito," she said while we walked home, "the Reyes Magos don't come to Cuba any more. They skip this island when they're on their route. They don't like it here. That's why I had to buy the toys myself." "There are no Reyes Magos," I said. "I've known it for a long time, Mami." She wanted to know who had told me such lies. "They're not lies, Mami. There are no Reyes Magos."

My most terrible memory. No. Not the beatings my father and my grandmother gave me. Not Father Castellanos. No, not the picture of Heaven and Hell that Grandma put in my bed, not that either. No, not the time when Amelia found out that I had been horsing around with her daughter. Not the rape. None of that. It happened the summer before we left the island. We had these relatives, an aunt and an uncle I had never seen or heard about. Pepe and Lulu, an older couple. They had connections in the States and they were going to help us get out, or get money for when we got up North, or something like that. They lived in Varadero, "the most beautiful beach that human eyes have seen." When Father decided we would leave the country, he started talking about Pepe and Lulu all the time. "We have to make sure that they know we care," he'd say. So he would send them big packages of food. All of a sudden, out of the blue, Father was a devoted nephew. He had managed to take us to Varadero once a year, during the summer, even through the roughest revolutionary times. He managed. He always managed. And never, until our last trip, had we visited Pepe and Lulu. We would rent a cabin in one of the nicest resorts and eat sumptuous meals and swim. The water was crystal clear and the sand looked like sugar. The only part of those vacations that I didn't like was when Papi would play rough with us boys, pushing our heads under the water and keeping them there until we couldn't breathe and we started swallowing water. But even that isn't my most terrible memory.

The last time we went to Varadero we spent an entire day trying to find a place to stay. Everything was full. It occurred to Father that we should visit our relatives before we headed to Santa Clara that same evening. Pepe and Lulu were older than I had imagined. They hadn't gone to the beach in years, Pepe said. They hated the water. How could they, I wondered. They lived in a small house in a residential barrio. In front of their house, across the dirt street, there was a large apartment building. "None of the people around here are tourists. They all work or have retired." Tía Lulu fixed us a delicious rice and shrimp dinner and, while we ate, Father told them about his plan to return home that same night. Tío Pepe told him that we could stay for as long as we wanted in their home. "Oh no," said Father, "we don't want to impose." "Nada de eso," Lulu insisted, "you're staying with us, and I don't want to hear another word."

Mother took over the kitchen and our aunt was happy about that. Lulu was fat and Spanish looking. Her hair was completely white and she smiled all the time. Pepe was younger than her. He was tall and still very strong for his age. He needed a special diet. He'd had part of his stomach removed because of cancer. Pepe took Johnny and me for a stroll around the barrio very early each morning. Then we would come back home, have a big breakfast, and go to the beach. But we couldn't get in the water right away, not until our food had been digested. So we built sand castles or buried each other and pretended we were dead. Or we'd run after the tiny crabs and catch them and squash them.

One morning, before anyone had gotten up, I was awakened by this voice, like moaning; it was a woman's voice. It got louder and louder and then I heard the sound of things being kicked and thrown, like furniture and stuff. I was surprised to find all the others asleep. The screaming was getting so loud! I got up and I ran outside the house. I looked in all directions. The street was empty. It was still dark and there were lights inside some of the apartments across from us. Then I saw the smoke coming from one of those apartments. I have never felt so terrified. I imagined the people inside, little children like me, burning. I thought I should do something, run inside and tell Father, but I felt paralyzed. A black woman appeared in front of me a few seconds later, not far from where I was standing. Her arms stretched out, far from her body. Naked. She was in flames, Erica. Fire was coming out of her breasts, her stomach, her legs. She cried. "Auxilio! Dios mío! Auxilio!" But I couldn't help her. Some people came out and threw blankets on her. I was still standing there when they put her inside this car and took her away. I heard Mother telling me to come inside, scolding me for having left my bed and for watching that scene. But I couldn't move. I just couldn't move.

A few days later we heard that she had died.

Dear Nito,

How are you? I have some good news and some bad news. The good news first? OK! I'm doin better in school. I have good grades and the teacher says that I am behaving better, she wrote that in the report and Papi and Mami bought me some records for behaving good. The bad news? Are you ready? Papi says that we have to get rid of Princess. He says we have to move to an apartment, a smaller house maybe, because we can't afford to stay here and because this house is too big for just the three of us, now that Johnny got married and you, well, you haven't lived with us for a long time. I told Papi, what about when Big Bro Nito comes to visit? He said you can sleep in my room, and I sleep with Papi and Mami. And I said, great, I'll give up my room for my Big Bro Nito any time.

I'm gonna miss my dog. Ive had her for two years, you know. But we can't have a dog in an apartment, Papi told me. And another thing. You know what happened the other day? Something horrible, Nito. Remember Johnny's birds, the two canaries? Well, you know he left them with us because Mami loved to hear their singing in the morning, and he said, why not, like a present, you know, he would leave them as a present for us, and so we kept them in that little room in the back of the house. Well, Princess is getting kind of weird, you know. The other day. Are you ready? The other day we got home from Zodys, Mami took me there to buy me some shoes, and like all the other times, I went straight to my room to play some music and Mami went to the backyard to check everything. And then I heard her screaming. I got scared, Big Bro! Can you imagine, my Mommy crying and screaming out there. I ran so fast! When I got there I saw Mami kneeling on the floor, by the cages of the canaries. And you know what? They were dead, and the cages were all broken up, and there was this big hole on the screen door, because Princess, she is weird, you know, she made that hole and attacked the poor pajaritos. Mami sat there for a long time and cried and cried. I didn't know what to do. I thought, I have to punish this dog, so I hit her, I told her she was a criminal. Mami said later that the birds died from the susto. They were frightened. Princess didn't bite them or nothing like that, she just frightened the poor little birds. I hit her. And I felt so bad afterwards. I felt really bad. So you see, we cant keep Princess. That's what Papi says. That dog is a bird killer, he says. We don't want no killers in our home. But she did it because she's young and she doesn't know better, right?

Well, I guess I have to go now. Im helping Mami put all the stuff in boxes. Next time you come we will be in another house. I saw the new house already. It's in Hawthorne too. And we get to keep the same phone number. I hope you like our new house.

Luv ya,

Geneia

STEP TWO

These Four Walls

"The city where we will be living in the North is named after a flower," Mother said when she found out that we would probably be sent to Gardena, where my uncle Paco lived. Most Cubans stayed in Miami, but we weren't one of the lucky families, according to Father. He wanted us to be far from his brother. No chance. They told us we had to go where there was family. Tío Paco was bigger and louder than my father. And he treated my parents like servants. He would walk into our apartment, which was in the same building as his on Vermont, and he would demand the key to Father's old Rambler, food, anything he fancied. He never stopped reminding us how he had helped us and put us up and found Father a job.

We began to hang out with the Jehovah's Witnesses. Father said that now we had new brothers. But after a couple of Bible readings, he got sick of the Witnesses because they claimed to be the chosen ones and all that stuff and they had bad tempers and were vicious and envious and jealous, just like everybody else. So he dropped them. But by now they had already gotten to Johnny, my lonely and desperate brother. "A good way to meet people," he'd say. "They have parties and girls go to them. Good girls. No drugs and none of that crap." Eventually Johnny would become one of the Kingdom Hall's proudest possessions.

When my grandparents arrived, a few months after us, Father rented a big apartment for the entire family. But he got into fights with Grandma every day, so he found them a tiny studio a couple of buildings down from us. Grandma Josefa and Aunt Lola, the "old maid," didn't leave Cuba until two years later. By the time they arrived, we were already living in Hawthorne and I was going to Leuzinger High. We moved to Hawthorne so that, as Father explained, I didn't have to go to Perry Junior, with all those niggers and mexicanos. My grandparents moved to Hawthorne, too. And eventually Josefa and Aunt Lola.

Grandma and Mother used to get mad at me when I spent a lot of time with Josefa. Their resentment went back to the days when Father decided to marry Mother. Apparently, the Toledos looked down upon the Fernández because they were poor campesinos and they lived in Zonalegre. But the Toledos were rather fond of Paco's pretty wife from Havana. Mother couldn't stand the fact that her mother-in-law loved her disgusting son Paco more than she loved Father. My dad, she claimed, was the one who took care of the two old women. How could they love Paco more? What did he ever do for his mother and sister?

Grandma complained that Josefa didn't care about anybody. "She thinks she's a dama. She expects Gladys and me to kiss her feet. When we used to go to Varadero, it was your mom and me who cooked. She thinks she's a lady because she was the wife of a Spanish merchant. Bah, look at her now, a refugee like the rest of us." According to Grandma, if you loved your children you had to devote your entire life to them. Josefa didn't measure up to her definition of love. Why did I spend so much time with her? Why did I show her my affection? Why? She made no sacrifices. She sat there and let her daughter Lola do everything for her. She didn't try to help her sons in any way. She didn't suffer because her other daughter, Rosaura, was still in Cuba. She was a selfish and lazy vieja.

I loved Josefa the way one loves a friend. "Josefa," I never called her Abuela, "what do you think of this barrio, isn't it quiet here? Can you believe how quiet everything is in this country?" She would agree. "I haven't seen any of my

43

neighbors yet. I miss the noise, the fiestas, the evenings when I would sit out on the porch and we would talk with all the people who passed by the house. This place is like a cemetery, Nito. These people are dead."

Mother and Grandma constantly reminded me that Josefa loved Paco's children more than me and Johnny. And yet, whenever Paquito or Martita or Liana had the chance, they would enviously rub my face in the fact that I was Josefa's favorite. I didn't believe I was her favorite. But I was the one she could talk to. And that's what my cousins resented. When Josefa died, Aunt Lola was taken in by my cousin Martita. Lola, the story goes, gave up her youth to raise Martita. And today she's expected to pay rent to her niece, to cook for her, to take care of Martita's son, and to clean the house. "Like a servant," she says, crying, "Martita treats me like a servant."

Liana was my brother's age. She was a beautiful girl. Tall, slender, long black eyelashes, light complexion, dimples. In the early days, before we moved to Hawthorne, Liana and I fantasized about getting married and having children. "Will you marry me someday, Liana?" "No. We're cousins." "Can we pretend then?" And we did, during one summer vacation, while her parents and mine were at work and Johnny, Martita and Paquito were out of sight. Sex, if you can call what we had sex, has never been as intense and real for me as it was with Liana. I loved her breasts, her long and solid thighs. I would smell my skin to find her smell, hours after she had left. One day her hand rubbed against my crotch. She took it away immediately. I held it and brought it back to my erection. I unzipped my pants and, as we kissed, she timidly grabbed my penis and pulled its foreskin back and forth to the point of hurting. In time, though, she became less nervous. We would caress each other, slowly, and she would let me stick my finger in her, and move it around, around, while she moaned and sucked in the air with her mouth open. We never went all the way, but we went pretty far. We would stretch out on the floor and take each other's organs with our mouths, hungry and thirsty. I would put my penis between her legs, being very careful not to penetrate her, and would move back and forth, biting her nipples. One afternoon, when we thought that Martita, Paquito and Johnny were at the store, Paquito found us in my bedroom, going at it, and after that, Liana rejected me with the same passion that she had loved me. To this day.

I was surprised that Paquito didn't react violently when he caught us in the act. Instead, he just told his sister to go home because he had to deal with me alone. He said he was going to tell my parents. I was going to be in deep shit unless. Unless what? I asked. "Unless you give me a chupada, or as many chupadas as I want." He was asking me to give him a blow job. I couldn't believe my ears. He was such a machito. Of course, by asking me to service him that way, he wasn't being less of a macho at all. Or so he thought. According to his father Paco, I was destined to be a puto. "You're not like the other kids," Paco would tell me when I'd come over to visit his children, "I think you're a mariquita. Real men don't sit that way, don't smile that way, don't stay at home studying and writing songs; they don't chat with the girls the way you do." His son Paquito, on the other hand, was destined to be a Don Juan, a ladykiller. Paco was livid when Paquito decided to drop out of school and get married. If his son didn't want to study that was fine, he didn't care, but he wouldn't allow him to get married. He was too young and hadn't known enough women yet. So Paquito eloped with his girlfriend Sonia. When he showed up one afternoon, holding his wife's hand, his father gave him such a beating that he had to be taken to the hospital.

I told Paquito that I didn't care if he told my parents. He reminded me about his father's temper. "Okay, so Tío Juan won't do anything to you, but my father will. Come on," he said. "I know you want to do it." He took out his thing and let it hang there, the ugliest penis I had ever seen. I told him I would only do it if he covered it with dulce, the mango preserve that Mami had made, for example, or sugar. I wasn't going to put that thing in my mouth just like that. The poor guy went to the fridge and took out the preserve and smeared it all over his member. "Like that?," he asked. "Will you do it now?" I told him to sit down, on the bed, and to take off his pants completely. His father was right, he must've thought, Nito really was a puto. I put the jar of preserve on the floor, at hand, and held his penis, which was long and hard by now. "Suck it," he said. I felt very awkward. I thought about what would happen to me if my family found out. But I did it. I put his penis in my mouth, and when the mango preserve was all gone, I didn't smear any more on it. His penis was the same size as mine. Makes sense, I thought. We're cousins. His hand pushed my head down on his erection, forcing me to take more and making me choke. I didn't have to suck for long. When he came in my mouth, I was sure I would vomit, but I swallowed his semen and sat back, hoping the nausea would pass. "If they made an x-ray of your stomach," he said as he put his pants back on, "they would know that you've swallowed a man's milk. They would know you're a faggot, a maricón." The third time that I gave him head, he asked me, "Do you get a hard-on when you're sucking me?" I answered, "Yes, like cement." He asked me to show him. I did. The fifth time, he asked me to beat off while I sucked him. The tenth time, he masturbated me. The last time we got together, a few days before my family moved away, I asked if he would suck me. He smiled and held my penis with a strong grip. "I'd really like to," he said, "but I'm a man."

Father believed that the best way for a boy like me to become a man was by working. "Julián, you've got to get a job. It's easy here, they let you work in the afternoons, after school, and on weekends." I walked a couple of blocks down Hawthorne Boulevard and found a Help Wanted sign at a Burger King restaurant. They needed an Opening Man. That meant getting up at five thirty in the morning, being at the store by six, assembling the machines, setting up the lard for the fries and preparing the mix for the shakes. Being Opening Man also meant having the store all to yourself in the morning, having at your disposal all the food you could possibly eat for breakfast. My favorite sandwich: whopper buns, two quarter pound patties, five slices of ham, gobs of mayo, mustard; all accompanied by dozens and dozens of fries, two, three chocolate shakes and three apple turnovers. When I began to notice the weight gain, I looked for another job. I ended up working as a meat apprentice at a supermarket. I worked there for a long time, until I had an accident. I was picking up some trash from the floor, papers and boxes, in the back room, when I felt this sharp object going up my arm, like a thick needle. There was a meat hook underneath all the trash. I ended up being taken to the emergency room and getting twenty stitches. After that, well, things got better. I graduated from high school and started taking classes at El Camino College. Biology, piano, voice, French, and English. I made some money tutoring English at the college's Learning Center. And I began to make plans for putting a band together.

Father got a job at the same factory where his brother worked. Micromize. Five dollars an hour! We were going to make it, he was sure. We were going to be able to buy nice furniture and rent a big house in some other city, far from Paco. Father had to lift heavy parts that were put into some machine. He hurt his back and was out of work for several weeks. That time was hell for him and for all of us. He was mad at the world and took it out on his family. Tío Paco tried to get him to sue the company so he could get lots of money and set up his own business, but Father refused. He wanted the company to pay for his medical bills and to hold the job for him, that was all. They did pay for some of his expenses, but when he felt better and asked to be taken back, they told him they didn't have an opening any more. He worked in two other factories after that, until he started painting houses, which he's still doing today.

Mother worked at first in a door lock factory. She would come home crying over her torn up nails and her bleeding fingers. She wasn't any happier when she started working at the International Testing Company. Her eyes hurt. She was losing her excellent eyesight because of the damned microscope. But she had no choice, Father said. He worked for himself and had no money for medical insurance. She had to stick it out; they needed the company's benefits. Mother remembers, nostalgically, the days when making a living was the task and problem of the men; when she could get up in the morning knowing that the housework would be done by the maid; when she could have breakfast at her leisure, and stay in bed while she listened to the radio-novelas. She doesn't need to work now, but she does. "I have friends at work," she says. "If I didn't have that job, I'd never see anybody. I'd have no reason to buy new clothes or to get my hair done. I'd never leave the house. I'd have no place to be but inside these four walls."

Dear Pegasus Julian,

How ya doin man! im doin okay over here hearing some metal and new wave. hey dude, you know what? im into punk rock and very much into heavy, too! i guess its just my age you know cause you told me you had a heavy age too. know what? im startin to like history cause instead of watching the tube at night i read some history.

You know theres this dude in my room who i really think is a nice dude. His name is Louis Consepsion. He likes punk and a little heavy metal. Well he is giving me his QUIET STRIKE tape for a buck! Hes a really smart dude, too.

You know i think Mrs. Morson is really going to like my report. Its a very intrestine subject. Lincoln is a wow fella to read about. I really liked readin about that dude. You saved my life, Big Bro, cause if you havent helped me with my outline, I would of been in trouble. I might turn into a manic depressive.

Hey when are we going to those museums youve been talking about? I want to go to the one in L.A. Remember, for my birthday I want to go to the science and industry one.

I luv ya . . .

. . . I miss ya

Unicorn . . .

. . . Geneia

Julian's Portfolio

Q: . . .

A: When I was in high school my main love was music. But the reason that I wanted to go into music was so I could be famous and make a lot of money, basically like any entrepreneur. I don't remember exactly when I started to change . . .

Q: . . .

A: I did *Godspell*. I played Jesus.

Q: . . .

A: My favorite song is "All Good Gifts." I also like "Alas Alas," which is about how Jesus criticizes the priests because they were hypocritical and materialistic and you know, the only way to be saved is through Christ and all that stuff . . .

Q: . . .

A: I'd had a really bad experience in church, back in Cuba, with a priest, you know, but that didn't make me hate Christianity. When we got to the States we went through a strange phase when we studied the Bible with the Jehovah's Witnesses.

Q: . . .

A: I didn't like them. I wanted to be a good Christian, but not if that meant going by the rules those people had extracted from the scriptures.

Q: . . .

A: My faith was strong in those days. You know, when I was playing the part of Jesus in *Godspell*, I really felt like I was doing the Lord's work. Before every performance—we did about seven—I would stand for twenty-five or thirty minutes backstage, I'd find a little place back in the wings, where nobody could find me, and I'd pray. I did, I really did.

(I put an ad in the paper and he answered it. That's a very strange way to go about getting an agent, he said. I had asked some of my classmates at El Camino but no one took me seriously. They thought I was joking or something. Why would I need an agent? What was he going to be my agent for? Did I think I was going to get jobs playing my lousy songs and pounding on those poor piano keys and singing like a Ricky Ricardo with laryngitis? Mrs. Enos, one of my voice instructors, what a witch. The woman would walk into the classroom puffing away on a More and This is the way you support yourself, down here, tighten up, come on, pretend that you're gonna be farting and then let it out, not the fart you idiot, your voice! I didn't dare to ask her for help. I did consult with Dr. Williams; he was tall, thin, bald and had kind eyes. Wonderful baritone. He didn't think I should be asking around for an agent. Learn your music. Get better. Then we can talk about an agent. There were people in Piano who were doing gigs and making a living from it. They didn't help me either. Their agents had too many clients already and they were only interested in experienced musicians, artists with a good portfolio. Portfolio, is that what they called it?

The Learning Center at El Camino paid me one thirty-five an hour, fifteen hours a week, for tutoring English, and provided me with a place to study, some resources, and a lot of encouragement in my studies. Joe Calderón needed help with his English 1A. He was Cuban too and he played the guitar. Tall and muscular mulatto. He must've been at least six feet tall. His hair fashionably Afro. His father had been a famous conga player in Cuba. Joe started playing with his father at the age of thirteen, during Carnival time. His whole family would dance and play music on top of a lush float, the Carroza, that his entire neighborhood in Guantánamo would spend a year building for the Parade. His mom was good, she was very good with the guitar. Hard to believe, he said, because she was a woman. She taught him chords and picking and a whole lot of songs. Now he was taking classes at El Camino, and doing part-time construction work. He lived alone.

We ended up spending our first meeting talking about the "possibilities." He could play guitar, congas, timbales, güira, palo. When we got really into practicing I asked him to get another tutor. I didn't want to talk about dangling modifiers and adverbial clauses with him. I wanted us to talk about music).

Q: . . .

A: There is something in me that seems to drive the motor that makes me want to write beautiful music.

Q: . . .

A: I've been a musician my whole life. I taught myself to play the guitar when I was very young. I took piano in college. Unfortunately, my parents didn't believe that boys should be taking piano lessons, so I started kind of late. Not long after forming the band I got a tutor. I would come in to see her and she would sit down at the piano and say, O.K., Julian, here's the piece that I want you to learn this next week, and she'd play it and she'd say, okay, see if you can play through that. Hell, I wouldn't even look at the music and I would just play back to her what she played to me.

Q: . . .

A: In college it was always YOU HAVE TO WRITE LIKE THIS AND YOU HAVE TO WRITE LIKE THAT. You can't do certain things because they don't sound good. That's when I started to see all the neat little theories that go into songwriting, technical stuff, you know. Like parallel fifths.

Q: . . .

A: You don't know?! A fifth is the outer interval in what's called a triad, your basic C E G, A C E, any three notes with thirds between them, a triad.

Q: . . .

A: Yes, and there are minor triads, major triads. It's

the outer portion of these three notes.

                da   and the fifth is   da
            da
You go   da   da
                                            If you had
three of these notes that you moved
you know   ba
                ba
                    ba

        and you wanted to move down to ba

                                        ba . . .

(The possibilities: We could practice in the garage at his
parents' house. He already had a bass guitar. I rented an organ. Someday our group would have a piano, a real piano,
like in the jazz bands. I could do the lead vocals, since I had
the training and a very "commercial" tenor voice. We needed
a drummer. There'd be no problem getting one. Joe knew a
lot of guys who wanted to jam. So Lucho Martínez, another
Cuban, joined us one Saturday afternoon. Lucho was short,
very thin and pale, and had long, straight black hair. He
didn't look any older than fifteen but he was about our age.
At first I thought he was wrong for our band. Too frail or
something. And was he really going to play those drums? Did
he have the strength? Hell, Karen Carpenter was skinnier and
weaker and she did fine. But then, we weren't going to be
making "Close to You" kind of music. We wanted real drum-
ming, loud and powerful and Cuban. During that Saturday
afternoon session Lucho proved to us that he was not only a
giant at the drums, but that he could also play the guitar and
the organ. He wasn't going to school. High school was all
right, he said; he had played with the orchestra during the

whole four years and had gotten to do a lot of neat shows. But now he was sick of school. He had a full-time job selling shoes at Shoe Rack and he spent most of his free time just playing his drums or his guitar. He was an only child. He still lived at home and was planning to do so for the rest of his life. His parents left him alone; he didn't have to pay rent and his mom cooked for him and did his laundry. He told us he had a lot of girlfriends.

Joe never said anything to me about Lucho, about Lucho as a person, that is. We did talk about Lucho's talents and about how good he was for our band. And to this day Joe pretends not to notice the glances that Lucho and I exchange. When we touch he just says, "You fucking faggots stop that shit and let's get some music going here!"

Now we wanted someone who could do many different things, like Lucho, but who gave his best as a sax player. This time we put an ad on the bulletin board in El Camino's cafeteria. We went through four or five American guys that we didn't like and then Roli answered the ad. He was Cuban, that was already a point in his favor. He was planning to get a degree in Law, and had studied and had been playing the sax for years. He was no Charlie Parker, but, Would we give him a chance? I remember thinking, when he got out of his car and walked towards the garage, holding his sax like it was a toy, how incredibly handsome he was, some Greek god, the epitome of Cuban masculinity. Roli never ceased to charm me with his classy posture, his reserved manner, his big green eyes that always seemed somewhat troubled. But he would never become as much of a friend of mine as Lucho.

Roli was very much into the "Cuban Scene." He would hang out with people from the Club Cubano of Glendale, where he was considered an excellent catch: good-looking, clean-cut, with the potential to become a wealthy lawyer someday, a charmer, a gentleman, a heartthrob. Roli continued to be faithful to his Cuban Club admirers for about a year, until a terrible rumor was spread in the circles that he frequented, something about what he really was behind his masculine facade: a disgusting invertido, a low-life homosexual who mingled with a rather ambiguous bunch—us. Then he dropped out of his Glendale Cuban Scene and started to pay more attention to his "ambiguous" pals. He didn't deny the rumor nor did he confess to being a homosexual. When some of our musical fantasies began to materialize, Roli abandoned his plans to become a lawyer and joined the band full-time. But on one condition, he said, that we never played in Glendale.)

Q: . . .

A: You see, a triad is root form. Three notes in it, each has a whole step in between, C E G, D F A, okay, on the scale. But you can invert this triad, first inversion or second inversion, which is, each time you take the bottom note of the triad and go up an octave, and you add it to the top of the chord, to make the first inversion. Then you take the new bottom note and go up an octave, to make the second inversion.

Q: . . .

A: What they don't want you to do is, you shouldn't have one triad right after another in a piece of music, you know, from here to here . . .

Q: . . .

A: Aha . . . in root position, because what it ends up doing is parallel fifths. And what happens when you move two chords successively from one place to the next then the outer portions of the triad are still in the 1-3-5 form with a fifth at the end. Well, to them, that sounds bad. Maybe it does, but in certain cases it can also be very effective.

(I didn't meet Amanda until later, when I already had the band. How does that story go? Amanda's sister, Lorie, was going to Hawthorne High, like Johnny. They were taking some classes together. My brother was invited to a party at her house and asked me if I would go. I did. And at the party I met Amanda. She had just arrived from El Salvador. She was here to study English. Her dream was to become a bilingual secretary. Amanda was as tall as me and a little on the chubby side. She had long frizzy hair and an innocent face. Her skin was dark. All her gestures seemed carefully planned. There was no doubt in my mind that she was a virgin. A virgin. My first virgin. I couldn't wait. But it took a long time. There were days when I thought to hell with you. Forget it. Then she would call or she would come over to bring me one of her Salvadorean rice dishes, specially made for me. And Grandma treated her like she was an angel that had suddenly fallen from Heaven. My entire family adored her. Meanwhile I was beating off thinking about Amanda's tits and her tight little cunt and her ass and the works. What a creep.)

Q: . . .
A: Some of my favorite composers were part of the Impressionist movement, Debussy, Rachmaninoff, Ravel. The ones that wrote beautiful dreamy music. I also love the Romantics, Chopin, Brahms. Mozart and Beethoven too, but they were more Classical . . .
Q: . . .
A: Those artists like Chopin and Beethoven, they wrote a lot of piano concerti. I love piano concerti. I could listen to them forever. I love the piano. You know, it's the most important musical instrument that was ever invented. Before it they had harpsichords, that's what they used during the Baroque

period, that real brittle Baroque kind of decorative sound.

Q: . . .

A: Yes, I also like some of the contemporary composers, Samuel Barber, Stravinsky, Aaron Copland.

Q: . . .

A: The composer I admire the most, throughout history? My all-time idol?

Q: . . .

A: No, that's not a difficult question. Wolfgang Amadeus Mozart. I wish I had lived in the late Eighteenth Century. I wish I had known Mozart. I would've been a very different Salieri, that's for sure. I would have worshiped Wolfgang Amadeus. I would've given up my life to serve him, to help him grow old, to make sure that he would write not 626 compositions, but millions. One thousand operas, five thousand symphonies, three thousand piano concerti, eight hundred thousand sonatas, thousands and thousands of arias. Yes, perhaps Salieri was right, perhaps God was showing Himself to us through that unruly and foolish boy who leaped over tables and turned somersaults right after performing his beautiful masterpieces. Perhaps then, had I witnessed His greatness through Mozart, I wouldn't have doubted His existence. I would have probably been a believer.

Q: . . .

A: When I listen to Mozart's Piano Concerto in D Minor, I drift into oblivion. I am no longer me. I am his. I am his music.

Q: . . .

A: Yes, I would like to write a symphony someday.

(Geneia had just been born so I moved out of my parents' apartment, to leave them more room, and I moved in with my grandparents. I made a deal with them that I would give them some money for rent and do their grocery shopping. One night Amanda and I went out to the Marina, to dance at Big Daddy's, and came home really late. Grandma and Grandpa were sound asleep. Amanda was a little drunk already. I got her to smoke some pot. Her first time. She got really weird on me. She thought she was going to die. I'm dead, Julian, I know I'm dead. This isn't me talking. Like I don't even know if I said what I just said. Did I really say that? I'm dead, Julian, please save me. I held her and kissed her and made love to her and she cried all night long. She had given in, she was doomed, she had lost it all, it was the end. She would never be able to get married now. Will you marry me, Julian?

We were together for two years. During that time she blossomed; she became a beautiful, fashionable and sophisticated woman. And I felt proud that I had taken her away from her provincial, Latin American bourgeois mentality and had shown her a world of risk and passion and glorious fucking. At the end of those two years she had fulfilled her dream. She had attended the Hawthorne Business School and had become a skillful bilingual secretary. I had already finished my A.A. degree in music, had built up a repertoire, was playing at parties and weddings, had cut a single, had appeared on Spanish International Broadcasting, and had gotten, thanks to my agent, a job in Madrid. The plan: she would go back to El Salvador and she would wait for me there. I would go to Spain, make lots of contacts, maybe even get a record contract, and go to El Salvador, to ask her parents for her hand. Then we would return to L.A., her favorite place in the whole wide world, and we would have an expensive, unforgettable and romantic wedding.

I didn't write to her during the nine months that I was in Spain. She wrote to me constantly, every week, some weeks a letter a day. She was waiting for me. All the plans were made. Why didn't I write? You creep.)

Q: . . .

A: I don't like the outrageous avant-garde stuff, like John Cage, that guy who sits for a while at the piano and then pounds on it. I have a hard time accepting that as art.

Q: . . .

A: Yes, I'm a real big fan of the early jazz, with just the string bass, the sax and piano. I just love the doong doong doong doong and pretty soon the sax comes in you know the piano's back there just playing jazz chords. That forties kind of jazz I guess you would call it.

(My agent. Yeah. That's how I met him, he answered my ad. He called and he said he had never worked with a client who had put an ad in the paper. He said he had good vibes about our group and he wanted to give us a listen. But first, since I was the musical director, would he be able to meet with me alone, and then we could arrange for an audition. If he liked us, he said, he would help us. So here I am, in Burbank, stoned out of my brain, in this lush bungalow, sitting next to a man of about thirty, stripped to his waist, tight jeans, barefooted, his hair black and sort of fluffy or disheveled, you know, and we're drinking Cuba Libres and listening to Pink Floyd and talking about how he really was a sound engineer, and that's how he could afford to live so well, how he wasn't going to be able to help me get into Angel Records, the firm that he represented, because you see, they weren't interested in young Ethnic. But that he knew the Spanish scene, he knew people in SIB and "that Spanish culture is growing, it's getting to be quite a business. You Latinos really follow the Lord's word, you know, you're multiplying." He would come up with some gigs, to get us started. We could do the New Year's Cuban dances, when all the Cubanos got down and you know, *Una dos y tres, Qué paso más fuerte, qué paso más fuerte!!* The night clubs on Pico and Broadway. He could send us to Union City, in New Jersey, and for sure we could work in Miami. In Florida we'd probably find a producer. Or, he could produce us himself, that is, if we were good and dedicated. And of course, only after we had paid our dues.

So here I am, asking this thirty-year-old Lee, the part-time agent, what he means by pay our dues. And there he is, the incarnation of Warren Beatty, telling me that he really liked his job, that he got a kick out of breaking in the new talents, opening doors, giving the young kids a chance to express themselves, to come out with their new and exciting sounds. I immediately knew he wanted to fuck me. I hadn't had it up my ass since the time I was raped in Zonalegre. So my first reaction was to get the hell out of there. He must've picked up on my feelings, because he leaned forward and gave me a kiss, a tender and loving kiss. Nothing wrong with that, I thought. Then his hand held the back of my neck, so that I couldn't move my head, and he licked my face, my chest with his tongue. I was hot like hell but still indecisive about what was to follow. I made a gesture to indicate I was still determined to go. "Just stay with me kid," he said. "I'm gonna help you, I promise. I'll get you a job and I'll even produce your first album. I promise." And I thought he was lying, but he wasn't. He meant every word.)

Q: . . .

A: I hear music. It's inside of my head. Sometimes I go to bed at night and as I'm lying there on the brink of consciousness, just before I fall asleep, I'll hear beautiful symphony music. And I always realize that I'm composing it, as it's going on in my head, I'm writing it. And I write in different styles, you know, sometimes I'll be doing hard rock, if I'm in a real radical mood, or if I'm real peaceful I'll be hearing strings and French horns and bassoons and I'll sit there and alternate the melody and all the parts and stuff.

Q: . . .

A: It's like I have this connection between the physical world and the dreamworld of my deepest innermost thoughts. And I'm completely uninhibited as I'm drifting off to sleep. Then daytime comes and I go and sit down at the piano and either the music just doesn't sound quite as good or I can't remember some of it.

Q: . . .

A: It appears as this kind of collage of notes. Fades in and out of notes. If someone were to wake me up at that instant, I could hum the melody to them. It's not just a dream.

(Lucho and I got together a few times while I was seeing Amanda. She knew it. When I left her to go practice with the band, she'd give me this look of disapproval. But we never talked about it. It was as if we had mutually and silently agreed not to discuss the "issue." If we spoke about it, everything would end, my relationship with her, with him. Everything.

She liked to criticize the men in her family and in her country. Cold, distant men, she would say. Men who have no feelings. Her father, an angry little dictator who spoke in one and two syllables. Amanda liked me because I wasn't like that, she'd say, because I was sensitive and caring and if I felt like it, I would cry. But she also wanted me to be a man with her, to order her around, to tell her what to do and to take her hard, to bite her and make her suffer, like a man, she'd say, because that was exciting. I haven't known any other woman to be as earthy as Amanda. In comparison, my Ericamor is a feather, a gentle bird. Amanda wanted pain).

Q:. . . .
A: I don't think technically through a one-four-five cadence, which is just a chord progression, it's more like I just start playing and . . . my hands take me where I'm going. I don't sit there and play a couple of notes and go, let's see now, I think the next part should go la la la la la. I play three notes and then I play seven more notes . . .

(Lucho was a lot like my cousin Paquito at first. He wanted me, but he wasn't sure and he had all this religious guilt to deal with and he was going to burn in Hell and God was going to punish us and our band wasn't going to make it. Yeah, he was sure that would be our punishment. No one would ever know or hear our music. I told him I didn't want to pressure him, and I was sorry if I had. "Hey man, we're partners, we're making music together, that's more important, no?" He didn't understand. He'd say, "I'm crazy about women, really I am . . . But I also like this other stuff, you and me, what we do together. It's weird, I'm only happy when I have . . . both. How do you explain that?" I knew exactly what it meant to be in his situation. But I had no answers for him.

When we came back from Spain, after making our first album, Lucho started doing a lot of guitar and helping me out with some of the writing. We ended up collaborating on most of the songs for the next L.P., *Family Portrait*, the record that was going to make our "statement." We had to stand up like the Chicanos, the Blacks and the Women and let ourselves be counted: "The kingdom of my parents/ the lost generation/ is in slavery, in obligation/ My kingdom is within/ in that Faraway Land which my shadow searches . . ." We were completely broke by the time the record came out, and when it did, it just sat there, no one heard about it, no one talked about it. No one played it . . . "Who knows it might be true/ we spend our lives attempting to fulfill the dreams we dream/ in the familiar space of memory . . ." It got very few and mixed reviews. But Lucho and I were better friends, better musicians, better lovers.)

Q: . . .
A: When I'm driving my car the first tape I look for is the tape that I'm hearing in my head at that time to evoke a fantasy. I'll pop it in and here comes this image of me up there playing, you know, aahh ahhh, the crowds going wild.
Q: . . .
A: Yes, I do want recognition. No one creates in a void.
Q: . . .
A: Maybe a desire for fame is somewhat of a weakness in character. For me it's not a choice. I feel compelled. And I don't fight it at all.

(Then I met Erica. The guys resented her at first. Did

she understand what we were doing? Like, had she heard of Bembé and Conga rythms, of Salsa? Did she know Tito Puentes, Celia Cruz, Willie Colón, Rubén Blades? Did she speak any Spanish? Could she sing "Recuerdos de Ypacaraí" and "Solamente una vez"? Or the Manzanero songs, or the more recent stuff like "Fui paloma, por querer ser gavilán"? No way, she was different man, she was radical, gringa, rockanrolera, almost punk and she probably snorted. We smoked some pot and we drank Cuba Libres but that was as far as we wanted to go. No junkies in our band. And what did I see in her, anyway? She was skinny, flat back and front. I could have any of those nice Cuban asses in Miami and Union City and I settled for that? So, she can sing and she knows people. So, she could make us famous. So, we could finally get rid of that good for nothing bastard that we had for an agent . . .

Are you so sure, Julian?

They didn't know her. They still don't know her. Yeah, they like her better now. They're learning things from her. She dazzles them with all that fancy studio technology that she can do. She's a great singer. She stands in front of a mike and she can make you cry, or she can make you the happiest being on Earth. When we did "Spring" we all felt like, you know, like she'd really become a shadow, a ghost almost, "It's bright outside/ and I'm a silhouette/ It's peaceful now/ and I have no regrets . . . I'm going now, my friend/ a fading silly silhouette . . ." Ericamor. My perfect lover).

Q: . . .

A: I would like for people to look back at my songs, let's say a hundred years from now, and I'd like for those songs to tell them stories, to describe for them our present world. And I'd hope that my songs would also be able, even then, to evoke an emotion . . .

Hey, Nito! Want to see the last ten videos? Here they are:

ARTIST	TITLE
MEN OUT OF WORK.........	I'M JUST HERE WAITING IN LINE
A FLOCK OF SEASLUGS	HELP ME MAKE IT THROUGH THE DOOR
EARTH, WIND, AND PARTLY CLOUDY.......	STORMY WEATHER
ABUTT COSTTELLO.........	DOES YOUR FACE HURT
ABUTT COSTTELLO.........	WELL ITS KILLING ME!
DEF SHLEPPER	MY NOSE IS IN LOVE WITH YOU
ZZ ZNOZE.................	HEY * WHO TURNED OFF THE LIGHT
DEXYS MIDNIGHT STUMBLERS	GET OFF MY FOOT
VULTURE CLUB.............	GET OFF HIS FOOT
BILLY JOKE...............	THE SHOWER CURTAIN
BILLY IRON...............	PUMPING IRON YELL

Hey, Nito! Ask a silly question . . .

HOW DO YOU LIKE SCHOOL? CLOSED
DID YOU GET A HAIRCUT? NO, I GOT THEM ALL
CUT.
DO YOU FEEL LIKE A GLASS OF MILK? NO, WHY?
DO I LOOK LIKE ONE?

WHAT DO YOU EXPECT TO BE WHEN YOU GET OUT
OF SCHOOL? AN OLD WOMAN.
IS IT COLD OUTSIDE? NO, WHEN I TURN BLUE
LIKE THIS, ITS USUALLY BECAUSE IM DOING A
SMURF IMITATION.
ARE YOU GOING TO BE LONG? NO, I THINK IM
GOING TO BE SHORT FOR A WHILE.
HOW CAN YOU GET SO DIRTY IN SUCH A SHORT
WHILE? PRACTICE, LOTS OF PRACTICE.

Hey, Nito! Some jokes . . .

WHY IS THE HAMMER SO SMART?—IT USES ITS
HEAD.

WHO IS YOUR SMALLEST RELATIVE—YOUR ANT.

WHY DO BIRDS FLY SOUTH—BECAUSE ITS TOO FAR
TO WALK.

The end of the Komikos.

Hey, Nito! I just thought of a super, totally awesome, radical, narly cool name for my group! SUPER-
CONFABULATION is that name. (Definition: A mixture of
noises). Do you think its a good name for my group? I do.
I know what kind of music my group could play, pop and
rock, right? Oh I almost forgot! How are you? And
everything over there? I'm fine, well just a little sick, I
mean I have a little cold, nothing to worry about. I am
getting excited about my group. But don't worry, it doesn't
interfere in my schoolwork.

You wont believe who my new idols are. It's a radical group called Duran Duran! I love the way they sing and play, and their so cute. Me and my friend Lauri Frances talk about them at recess all the time. She wants to marry them! I do not. She some times drives me nuts! Well I think I should say by-by cause my neck and fingers kinda hurt. By-by!

Love, Geneia the Komika

The Family Tape

(Drum overture)

Johnny: Ladies and gentlemen, Johnny Toledo! Hey Jul, what's happening, how's it going man?!! This is your brother! Your crazy brother. As you know uh . . . I gave me a kind of introduction there. How do you like it? Hey man, everything around here is the same old routine. Uh . . . Geneia is next to me right now and she wants to say a few things, but she's thinking, you know. And Mami's just looking at me with a big fat smile. Uh . . . Finally! She wants to say something. Listen. Talk, mija, go, talk. Come on! Tell Big Bro. How are you Big Bro Nito?

Geneia: How ah you Big Bro? I want a big coat for Mami too. Mami no have one . . . like mine . . . I wuv you . . . wuv you Big Bro Nito . . .

Johnny: Nito, she's kind of shy, so I have to catch her when she doesn't know that I'm recording. So you wait till later on. Uh . . . Uh . . . right now I'm kind of sad in a way because I keep lookingfor a job and it's hard to find one, you know, and I want to get married and until I have a job I can't get married. But I'm sure that with the help of Jehovah I'll find a job soon . . . The recordings you sent were great. I especially liked the song you wrote for our sister.

Hot line hot line, calling on a hot line. Operator, this is only for my baby to hear . . .

Johnny: Hey Jul, that was a song by the Silvers, one of the new songs here, "Hot Line," it's pretty good. Later on I'll play the tape you sent, with the hits that are popular there, for background music, you know. Hey, I can't believe so many songs are in English. Sorry if the sound isn't that great, 'cause I'll have to use Mami's recorder, the one she bought for her lessons. By the way, she's learning a lot. I'm sure she's gonna tell you about that later . . .

Geneia: Brown bear brown bear what do you see . . . I
see a little pink flower looking at me . . .

Johnny: Sing more, for Nito. Sing . . .

Mami: She can do "Guadalajara" real well. Come on,
Genny!

Geneia: Guadalajara es un llanoooo . . . México es
una lagunaaa . . .

Johnny: Hey! That's great!

Mami: Qué lindo!

Johnny: Do you remember the song "Eres tú"? How
does it go? Eres tú, como el agua de mi fuente . . .

Geneia: He sing bad, Mami . . .

Johnny: Eeeeeeeres tú, el fuego deeee miii hogar.

Geneia: Old McDonald had a farm, eee ah ee ah
oh . . .

Johnny: Do you like to drink milk?

Geneia: Yes, I do.

Johnny: You do! . . . Do you like to play?

Geneia: Why he is asking questions, Mami? I can sing
better than Johnny. I know "Guantanamera" in English. You
wanna hear? Guaaa, jeee, meeera, wooah . . . heee . . .
meeera . . .

Johnny: Guantanamera, guajira guantanamera, guantanamera, guajira guantanamera . . .

Geneia: In English, Johnny, in English!

Johnny: Wuntunuhmeruh,   Whuheeruh   Wuntunuhmeruh . . . Like that?

Geneia: There was a butterfly in my room . . .

Mami: And what's a butterfly doing in your room?

Geneia: She come in from outside, from the patio.

Johnny: Genny, you know Big Bro Nito is in Spain. He
is so lonely out there. Why don't you tell him something to
make him feel better, huh? Do you still love him, eh . . . Hey
Jul, she's talking a lot for a three year old, don't you

think? . . .

Can you hear the drums, Fernando? I remember long ago another starry night like this. In the quiet light, Fernando, you were humming to yourself and softly strumming your guitar . . .

Abuela: (Reading) Nito, I listened to your beautiful recordings. I am glad that you are making friends there in Spain and getting famous. I saw the pictures too. You seem so happy. May God be with you and may the Virgencita del Cobre save you from any evil . . . Well, Nito, I've got the chicken pox, at my age, can you believe it? The rug you sent me is so pretty and it goes so well with the furniture . . . . Also, the coat you sent the baby, every one who sees it says that it is a work of art. And Genny, when Gladys went to take it off her she put up a big fight, she didn't want no one to take it away from her. It's from Big Bro Nito, she said. Well, Nito, many kisses, many hugs, many greetings to all of your friends out there . . . Mwah, mwah . . .

Misty silence of the early morning. All around another day is dawning. Goodbyes ain't easy, so no one sees me when I go. I'm on my way. Remember yesterday? . . .

Abuelo: (Reading) Hello, Julián. How are you? I'm glad that you find yourself well. I am very well too, especially now that I stopped smoking. After all these years I realized that it was hurting me. I hope you stop smoking too, since you're younger and it would be easier for you now. You have a lifetime ahead of you. Quit now, Julián. Well, here goes a big hug from your grandfather who loves you . . .

I remember your face and the first time we kissed. How you started to blush, what you said when you touched my hand . . . And the drives to the beach, with the sand on my feet . . . I'd live it all again . . .

Papi: What happened, Julián? How are you getting along with those Madrileñas? I wanted to tell you, I received a letter from your girlfriend Amanda. She says she misses you and hasn't received a letter from you in a long time. Write to her soon, Nito, don't be a cabrón. She is a good woman and she loves you. I wish you success in your work. Your father, Juan.

Johnny: Hey Jul. Papi wants to know what kind of music Amanda likes. He wants to buy her some records because she was always so nice to our family. He says that it is probably very difficult to find good music in El Salvador and he wants to do this for her to make her happy. So, when you write, tell him what kind of music she would like. I told him that maybe any American songs would be fine.

Because I love you more than words could ever say, I can live again with no regrets of dreams that died before you came. Because I know this time this love is really mine, I can love again and touch the stars that seem so very far away . . .

Abuela Josefa: Julián, I am talking to you from my apartment, in Hawthorne. Oye, I wish you happiness this Christmas. May you have a rich and beautiful and happy Navidad. I am glad that you're having fun in Spain. I always wanted to go back, and so did Toledo. We never did. In his last days he mentioned his little town in Andaluc!a every minute, and he described it like he was there. He talked about his family and the plaza and the kids he used to play with. He said the weather was always warm in the South. Is it cold in Madrid? I always wanted to see Toledo's home town, but it was so expensive to travel to Spain. When my mother was dying I wanted to go see her; we already had four children and we were barely making it, so I couldn't. Now you're in the land of my parents, in the land where Toledo was born. I hope you like it and I hope you go see that little village near Seville where he grew up . . . I got a letter from Amanda. She's fine. She talks a lot about you. She is happy that you're succeeding in your music . . . There really isn't any bad news, just the usual, my aches and pains; I'm almost eighty you know. And your father and his brother Paco they still argue and fight and when they run into each other at the store they don't even look at each other. I am glad that you get along so well with Johnny. Brothers shouldn't fight. I love all of my children and I know that Juan is a very special son, but he should be more forgiving. Paco can't help being selfish and loud. He is a typical Toledo. Well, my love, I wish you happiness. Have fun in Spain and keep chasing your dreams.

Tía Lola: Hi, Julián, how are you? We received your letter and we're glad that you're doing well. You say that you're spending Christmas in Mallorca with friends. And you say that after Mallorca you're planning to go to . . . to . . . What's that place, vieja, the place that he's going to after Mallorca?

Josefa: The Canary Islands.

Tía Lola: The Canary Islands, yes. In January. We also received a post card from Amanda. She says she's lonely in El Salvador without you. She says that she likes being with her family, but that her family now is you and us, here in Los Angeles, not in El Salvador. She wonders if you're mad at her, because she hasn't heard from you in a long time. What should we tell her when we write to her? Are you planning to go get her and bring her to live with you? . . . We see Geneia everyday; Gladys brings her. Geneia says you taught her how to dance and sing. She is a good singer. She will probably end up in the music world just like you . . . Merry Christmas!

It's sad (so sad). It's sad, sad situation. And it's getting more and more absurd. It's sad (so sad). Why can't we talk it over? Oh it seems to me that sorry seems to be the hardest word . . .

Geneia: You know what, Big Bro, they're calling me stupid! Nito, I wuv you very much. I want you to come back home very fast. I miss you. Mami is going to buy me many dolls and I want you to see them when you come back. Bye Bye . . . Eres tú . . .

Johnny: Well, Jul, that was all I could get out of her.

I'm sure that you'll be very impressed when you hear her sweet little words. Right now she's in my room pretending that she is playing the trumpet. She's something else. I don't blame you for missing her. To tell you the truth, I had to go through hell to get these recordings, especially from Abuela and Abuelo, they had to write everything down first, and then had trouble reading their own writing! I hope that . . . you enjoy hearing from us, and . . . get back real soon. And . . . keep up the good work!

Tonight, does it have to be the old thing. Tonight? Oh, it's late, too late to chase the rainbow that you're after. I'd like to find a compromise and place it in your hands. My eyes are blind, my ears can't hear. Oh and I cannot find the time. Tonight . . .

Mami: Nito, I just came back from school . . . I am taking English. I can carry on long conversations with the other students now and I'm not so afraid to speak with the clerks in the stores and the American neighbors . . . I want to thank you so much for the beautiful coat you sent the baby . . . When I opened the package and she saw it I had to let her put it on, and then there was no way to take it off her. Your package arrived Friday the 26th, we were just about to leave for Zodys, Johnny, the baby and me, it was very hot, 78 degrees, but even so there she went with her heavy coat and her purse . . . she was soaking in sweat the whole day . . . Before I forget, I listened to your recordings. You know I'm very proud of you, Nito, you're so young and already you're making a record in Spain and traveling to so many places. I love those songs, especially the one you wrote for Genny, "Hermanita." It's beautiful, it made me cry. (She cries) Don't forget to dress warm, you're not used to the cold. Don't get sick over there, I can't go and take care of you, although I would if I had to, you know that. Well, my love, I don't have to tell you how much we all miss you and that we wish you all the happiness in the world . . .

Hi Nito! How r ya? How's it going over there? Sorry I took so long to write, but it's just UN-B-LIVE-ABLE (Cuban people say that a lot) the homework I have, not even the first month and we just turned in 3 compositions!

The first thing people ask me is "How's school?" Well, I'll tell you how's school, school is fine, it's the teachers who are retarded around here. Just today I gave my Math paper to my teacher and then she goes to me "Genny I can't find your paper and you are going to lose points." And I look at her like if I would say "Ho! Wait a minute Honky, I gave you the stupid paper!" I tell you I'm really mad! Gee, I better calm down. I sure do get carried away, huh?

Hey you know what (You say "No. What?") Their going to show "Cantarás Cantaremos—How it was made" on t.v. and I'm going to tape it. I tell my friends at school that you almost got picked to be in it. You should've been in it, Nito, like MIAMI SOUNDS. You know their Cuban too? Your songs are better than theirs thou.

Have you see any movies lately? I haven't. During the week my parents don't let me and on the weekend we just stay home. (By the way Dad is taking it easy over here). I'm starting to dress up more because I lost 10 pounds and now i'm size 8 I used to be size 12-14 in other words I used to fit perfect in my mom's pants. I weigh 130 and I used to weigh 140. Oh, and remember that bladder problem I used to have? Well I guess it was all SY-KO-LOGIK-AL.

What's your favorite group now? (Well, other than Julian and the L.A. Scene). Hey, have you heard that song by Cheech & Chong "Born in East L.A."? In the beginning he's talking to the cop who pulled him over and the cop says "Where were you born, man?" and he goes, "Huh, where was I born?" That's one of my favorite songs now.

Well say hi to all your friends for me because anybody who's your friend is mine. Oh and don't forget to say hi to Lucho and Joe and all the people in your band. And to your agent too. You know, he looks more like a rock star than you do! Where did you find him?! And by the way, when you're singing in concert, if there's a guy that's about 20 to 25 and has strong muscles, tan, cute, tell him to send me a picture and I'll autograph it for him. Ha! Guess your little sis isn't too little anymore.

I love you,

Dynamite Cuban

The Hardest Word

(A place of) narrow streets and old buildings. A car which lets you (one, us) see the Cibeles through the window. Their (his) quiet presence on the other side of the seat . . . *You were humming to yourself* . . . (A church of) majestic Spanish towers. *And softly strumming your guitar* . . . Arriving, tired, at a crowded airport (A tired arrival at a crowded airport). An alley (full) of balconies and rusty iron railings. A wall of bricks and flowerpots (Flower-pots on a brick wall). A ham and cheese sandwich (Bocadillo?), a beer, a fat waiter and a dirty apron. A leather overnight bag: our baggage? Wandering up and down unknown (strange? unfamiliar?) streets. Trusting blindly the name and number on that crumpled (bit of) paper: Our hostel in Madrid. An unlit corridor (hall) smelling of cockroaches. A slippery handrail. A tall red-headed woman leading us to a window which opens out onto a world of burned gas and smog. A dark room where dampness overwhelms me. Lips whispering words I can't understand (Spanish words murmured softly into his ear).

Changing into clean and wrinkled clothes. In silence . . . *Misty silence of the early morning* . . . A hard push towards the door. Total absence of words. Sweaty hands, a moist upper lip. A place swarming with cars, buses; mannequins in bright colored dresses. Neon screens projecting (myriad) artifacts and frozen smiles. Endless walking taking us to the other end of the street, away from the commotion, towards our gig in Madrid. Rhythmic movements which get us through the crowd . . . *Because I love you more than words could ever say* . . . The club owner has silvery hair. She's leaning on a jukebox in the middle of the room. She rushes to greet (meet) us. Her Castilian mouth (accent) spits out the rules of our contract. A man laughs like a cartoon villain. A double chin. He seems to be telling jokes. A shorter man caresses a tall, skinny glass. A woman lights a cigarette. She fills the room with smoke. She blows it into my eyes when I (pass) go by. A fat man with sunglasses climbs the stairs to which Silvery Hair is leading us. Loud noises come from a corner (of the room). *I can love again* . . . The sound of breaking glass. A girl in a black mini-skirt and a striped red and black blouse, knee-high boots, speaks to us, the Gringo (Cuban?) musicians. Ready to whip out the hits. *And touch the stars that seem so very far away* . . . I trip over a man with baggy pants, belt hidden by his belly. He's drinking a red-orange liquid. He tells Silvery Hair a secret. She laughs . . . We reach our (dressing) room.

It's sad (so sad). It's a sad, sad situation. And it's getting more and more absurd . . . A few days later: An unlit hall which ends in a room smelling of dirty clothes. *And it's getting more and more absurd* . . . She: a featureless face. A smell of armpits and gardenias. Gray stockings. Curly hair. And a small waist. He (Lucho). And I. (I) hide in a corner and lean (recline) on a small table. My elbow hits a lamp and it falls to the floor. *Sorry seems to be* . . . She looks at me. Naked breasts. Big white breasts (Breasts big and white). He has taken his shirt and shoes off; (He) keeps his pants on. She sits up on the bed and calls me. I say no with my head. He pushes me and orders me to kiss her. *The hardest word* . . . I tell him I'd rather wait until she has finished ('til she finishes). Finished with what? he asks. Finished undressing, of course. They both laugh. She removes her skirt and reveals a very tight girdle. It seems to choke her. Dark stockings come up to her thighs. She smiles at me. She lies down. She has beautiful eyes. He goes up to her and kisses and caresses her, (he) touches her breasts, (he) hides his head between her legs and remains in that position for a long time. *The hardest word* . . . She stretches her hand out to me. *The hardest* . . .

Tonight, does it have to be the old thing? . . . I lie down next to her. I touch her legs. Warm. She tells me to continue (not to stop), to kiss her. I do it. A taste of peanuts, alcohol and tobacco. (With a slight motion) she guides me to her breasts: (Emanations of) armpit and Maja perfume. He looks at me. *Oh, it's late, too late to chase the rainbow that we're after* . . . I watch him out of the corner of my eye. He is stark naked. She makes my mouth travel up and down her body. She makes me stop (at one point) when I reach the zone between her legs. I withdraw on first contact. Her hand presses (down) on my head. I make an effort. (S)he says Yes, that is good. And he draws near to kiss her. Then she pushes me away and opens her legs wide, so wide I fear she will split in half. He moves away. She draws me to her breasts. (She) embraces me. I'm on top of her now. She's very excited. She throws her head back. She moves (shakes) from head to toe, like a snake (like many snakes). Her fingers tickle my back. She breathes harder, deeply. *My eyes are blind, my ears can't hear* . . . He puts a pillow underneath her waist and throws himself on her. His legs have small black curls, like little ringlets. *Oh and I cannot find the time* . . . I close my eyes. I see myself embracing him. (His chest of black ringlets.) She moves faster. She screams softly many times. Then he moves away, falling at her side, short of breath (breathing hard). His chest and his stomach two balloons that inflate and deflate. I caress his chest and I embrace her. My throat feels dry; my tongue too (She's biting it!). I move with her, the way she wants it, while my hand reaches out and sinks in that other chest. In his stomach. His navel. His mouth. And (s)he moans. *Does it have to be the old thing?* . . . A (shuddering) sensation forces me to move furiously, faster, faster, faster. My sex. Where is it? *The old thing* . . . I feel sweaty and sticky. *Tonight* . . .

Dear Nito,

What's up? How's life in Orange Juice Florida? Do you like Miami? Papi says that its just like Cuba. Sorry I haven't written in such a long period of time. It's just that I've been trying to excel in school and there's a program I joined for helping the proletariat plus the newspaper, I've got my own column now, how do you like that? Maybe I'll be a writer. That's as good as a musician, no? So I come home at 4:30 then I stay up til 10:00 or 11:00 at night studying. The only time I have for leisure is on weekends and holidays. I'm not that lazy kid you used to know. I went from a D to an A. That's a pretty drastic change huh?

I bet your thinking, "Why is Geneia using those fancy new vocabulary words like proletariat?" Well I'll tell you BRO! I don't usually use them at home, but I use them at school all the time. I got some from this brain-racking book I'm reading entitled 1984. It's very interesting. I'm also reading VILLAGE OF THE VAMPIRE CAT. No, it isn't a horror story! It's about a Ninja. If you don't know what that is it's an unemployed Samurai.

Alright enough about books. I got a new group at school. Well, more like a duo. It's hot! It consists of Gabriela González and me. We thought our real names were BLAAH so we changed them to Gaby M. and G. the Dreamer. We also thought of calling ourselves DELIRIOUS. You like it? It's maximum raging, no? I'm really cool at school. Everybody knows who I am. I'm raging at school, DUDE. Just wait til I'm in 8th grade!!

G.

Where Is My Sebia?

She gets up at six or six thirty each morning. If he's awake she phones Juan. Then she makes coffee, very sweet the way Juan likes it. Juan gulps down the coffee and goes to Raúl's bedroom. He unties the old man and pulls him up by the arms, forcing him to stand up. He takes off his pajamas and the diaper. Raúl stands trembling, skin and bones. Juan pulls him into the bathroom. "He's like a mule, this man. He's stronger than me! Vamos, Raúl, don't make me work so hard." In the bathroom, Juan will push him down on the toilet. "There, take a shit." By now, Eusebia's ready with the washcloth and the medication for the sores on her husband's back. Juan holds his hands while Eusebia cleans his private parts, his back, his legs. No matter how warm the water is Raúl rejects it. "Stand still, Raúl! Let your woman do her job." She dries him off and puts cream in between his cheeks, where the skin is raw. "Ay," he cries. "Don't hurt me please." Juan pulls him back to the bedroom, where Eusebia searches for a clean diaper. Juan puts it on him; then the wool pajamas. Raúl is dragged across the living room, to his chair. Juan pushes him down again. "Down, Raúl, sit down!" Eusebia brings two pillows. Raúl rests his head against them. He opens his eyes when it is all done and he's left alone. He seems lost and confused. His right arm goes up and he lets it drop with all his might. He beats his hand against the side of the chair once, twice, ten times, screaming each time Coño, coño, coño, coño!

He falls asleep. Then Eusebia fixes breakfast. Cereal and warm milk for him. Coffee and toast with cream cheese for her. She pulls up a chair next to Raúl and touches him on the arm. "Time for breakfast." She goes to the kitchen and puts the cereal and the warm milk in a bowl. She holds the bowl in one hand and with the other touches him again, this time on his forehead. "Pobrecito," she murmurs. "Vamos,

Tabaquito, wake up and open wide. Eat your breakfast." She fills the spoon to brimming and stuffs it in his mouth, swiftly and aggressively. "It's quite a job to feed him," she tells Nito. "You've got to do it that way, otherwise it would take forever. But he likes his food. He eats well. I fix him good meals. When he had sores on his gums I had to put everything in the blender. Poor Raúl, eating mush all the time . . ."

After breakfast she turns on the radio, K-Love Radio Amor, and listens to the news. She never misses it. If she feels tired she rests on the couch for a few minutes while she thinks about the family, always about the family. Then, if it's a weekend, she calls Gladys to tell her about the horrible news she heard on the radio. If it's a week day she sits by the phone from approximately eleven to twelve, until her daughter calls from work during lunch hour. If Gladys doesn't get to the phone right at noon Eusebia runs to her bedroom and kneels in front of her saints. She won't get up until she hears the phone ring. Or, if it's one of those times when Gladys has gone to the mall, until she hears her car pulling in the driveway. "Yes, he's fine, he's resting now. I fixed him a good breakfast. Yes, I slept well. And how are you, my love? Are your eyes hurting you? You should ask to be put in another department. That microscope is burning your pretty eyes away. I worry about you, working so hard and having to drive out there in those streets full of locos and drug addicts. Ta bien, ta bien, I won't nag. But try to get transferred. I don't want you losing your sight for a miserable paycheck."

She feels at peace now. She can go back to the couch and collapse until it's time to cook lunch. She thinks about Nito. She loves all her children with the same passion and fear. But Nito needs her more. Since he was a little boy, when she fed him the way she feeds Raúl now, when she changed his diapers and then later, when she dressed him up so elegant and took him with her to visit her neighbors. She always felt proud of her grandson. He was so handsome. She knew he needed her. He was weak and sensitive, too sensitive for a boy, they said. Most of the neighbors loved her, but there were those who hurt her when they talked about how pampered he was, about how he would probably turn into an invertido. They were envious, claro. They didn't have an intelligent boy like Nito. She had never loved anyone the way she loved Nito. And she had never feared for anybody the way she feared for him. She knew why. He was alone. No one took care of him when he was sick. He didn't have a wife. He was artistic.

She's glad that she remembered to take out the chicken from the icebox this morning, before Juan arrived. She's going to make fricasé, with lots of potatoes that she will mash and make into purée for Raúl, and a nice salad. They haven't had avocado in a long time. Maybe next time the kids go to the store she'll ask them to bring her some. And she needs some of that Sara Lee pound cake that Raúl likes so much. "That's so good," he says, "delicious. Who made that? You made that, Eusebia?" Eusebia. That was the only name he remembered. He cried when he didn't hear the quick thumping of her feet around him, when he didn't hear her racket in the kitchen, or the bottles and plates and glasses that she dropped once in while. He cried when he looked for her and didn't find her. "Sebia! Sebia! Where is my Sebia?!!"

She had forgiven him long ago, even before Gladys was born. She wasn't about to go through life holding grudges against her mate. And she wasn't going to disgrace herself by running away and leaving him. But how she hated him in the beginning; his brothers, his father, how she hated them all. How they made her work and treated her like trash, like a servant. "Sebia, more water!" "Sebia, what happened with that yuca you said you were bringing?" "And the rice. We're almost out of rice." "Go, Sebia! Go and fetch us the food!" He never beat her. She was lucky for that. It happened to some of her sisters and friends. The husbands, all of them campesinos, took out their miseries on their wives. And there was no one to run to. No one to ask for help. If anything went wrong with the marriage, it was the woman's fault, not the man's. Always.

She wanted Gladys to be happy, to have a rich home and to enjoy life. Gladys needed to leave the barrio, she needed nice clothes and a refrigerator full of steaks. They couldn't give her any of that. No way. But Juan turned out to be worse than Raúl. She found her baby crying one morning, because he had hit her. She helped her pack and took her back with her. And she swore she would kill him if he showed up at the door. She was so sorry to have let her little Gladys marry Juan. So very sorry. Raúl did nothing but scream at her and blame her for their daughter's misfortune. Then one morning Gladys said she wanted to go back to her husband and her home. Eusebia tried to stop her. She begged her. She said my love he's violent, he'll hit you again. That type of man doesn't change. But she went anyway. Then came the children. And then it was too late.

For dinner they could have leftovers. She hardly ate. She liked the rice; she ate that in big spoonfuls. Raúl was a big eater. He had been a big eater all his life. He worked so hard. Raúl was an intelligent man, everybody said so in Zonalegre. He could fix anything, the pipes, the lights, the toilet. He was a good carpenter, too. The richer neighbors, the ones who had a bathroom, called him once in a while for repairs, on Sundays, when he wasn't working in the sugar cane fields. She never understood how he managed to fix cars; he never owned one and never went to school to learn about motors and those things. Whenever Juan had car trouble he came running to Raúl. And the car always worked after her Tabaquito spent some time playing around under the hood.

She's going to fix a roast for the kids on Sunday. Maybe Gladys could help her and they could invite Johnny and his family and have a big fiesta, for no reason, just to have all of her loved ones together. But Nito. No. She couldn't have a feast without Nito. When she first arrived from Cuba she couldn't eat meat or fancy food, she still remembers. She'd start eating and she would immediately feel a lump in her throat and in her stomach. She'd have to stop. Images of her brothers and sisters in Santa Clara filled her mind. They were hungry, she knew. It wasn't fair for her to be eating well while they went hungry over there. Hungry. Before and after Castro. That was the story of her people.

A feast on Sunday. She'd make the mojo for the roast the night before and she would put the meat in the oven real early, to cook all morning, and then for lunch . . . But Nito. She couldn't have a feast without Nito. Why was he away so much? Why had he become so cold and so distant through the years? She called him when he was out there in New Jersey, when he first left, and he hardly spoke on the phone. Like she was a bother. And he told her not to call him so much. "Call me once a week, Abuela, or wait for me to call you. I'm not always in the mood . . ." Not always in the mood, he'd say. Then once or twice a month he would call her. She'd pick up the phone and hear the voice she loved more than anything in the world. "How is my vieja doing, eh? My ugly vieja." And she would always respond the same way, "Your vieja's getting younger and prettier every day."

No more, she thought. It was time for him to come back home. This evening, when Juan came to put Raúl to bed, she would ask him to write to Nito. "Tell him we need him, Juan. Tell him it's urgent. Do anything you have to do to get him back here with us. Make him come back, Juan. I miss him."

Dear Nito,

How ya doin? I'm reading a whole bunch, getting 100% on most of my papers, and listening to tapes and records. I haven't seen any movies lately cause of Dad and his money but I'm in luck, Old Towne Mall movies are 1.00 again and I got discount tickets from the International Testing Company from Johnny, Oopps, I forgot to tell you! Didn't you hear that Ma is going to work where Johnny does? You know somthin' my Xmas vacation is until the 20-1 of January so we can spend lots of time together!!

I'm not into Breaking anymore but if you want me to break for you, sure, I still know how! I'm into Heavy Metal, Hard Rock, New Wave, and your music too! I forgot to tell you! The other day we were in the car, you know, and your song came on, "Family Portrait," and it was awesome, Nito, my own bro on the radio! Mami turned it loud and Papi got mad. You know, he hates loud music. My favorite song right now is "You're dogged up and we're not," by EVIL SISTER, my favorite group. Is your band going to play heavy metal some day?

I'm very interested in U.F.O.'s nowadays. I just came from the library and got a whole bunch of books on the subject. Do you know anything about Extraterrestrials (Sp?). If you do let me know!

You should see Andie! HE IS SO CUTE!! When he sees me he goes crazy! He starts jumping, screaming, and showing his little cute smile. I'm waiting for the other one now. It's due any minute! I hope it's a boy or a girl, how about you? (little joke there). Laura is pretty fat. If it's a girl her name is going to be Paola and if it's a boy we still don't know.

Well I guess that's it Nito. I can't wait till you come so I can hug and kiss you. I owe you a lot of hugs by now.

I LOVE YOU NITO!!

Geneia

You're My Son

There, we're almost there, go, faster, go Raulito, run, we're almost there. Up higher, to the top, shake all that good palmiche down, all of it, higher Lito, there, to the top. "Pipo, Pipo. How are you, viejito? You're feeling better? Is Mima giving you your food and your medication? Ah, Tabaquito? Yes? What is it? What do you see out there? There's nothing out there, viejito. Just a wall. Look, I'm touching it, just a wall. Don't be afraid." Look at me. Like this. Your knee on its neck, you'll find the heart right here. Hold the handle tight, yes, that's my boy. Then with strength all the way in. Feel the blood, the warm blood. You did it, Lito, I knew you could do it. Drink the pork blood, yes, you can, your brothers are doing it, look, they like it. It's warm and it tastes great. "Raúl! Time for a walk! Vamos, come on! Up, up. Así. Now walk a little bit. No, no, not that way. Grab him, Genny! Raúl, you stubborn old man!"

Faster, faster! I dare you! No, not like that! Let it know you're the master. You got to let the horse know. Don't let it go. Yes, like that. Let's see who gets there faster. Lito will. I know he will. He's my son! "He's going to hurt himself, Juan. You better sit him down again. He's going to fall." So many birds. Tiñosas!! Where do they come from? Coño. Coño. Go away. Sebia, the birds. Coño. They poke at him. Tiñosas. They make him bleed. Ay. Tiñosas. Shit. "A little water, Raúl? Some 7-UP? It's almost time for his dinner." Inside, now they're inside, on the right side. Coño, coño. Inside, grab them, like that, sí, that way. No no no! They're slippery. I can't grab them! "He must be hungry, I can tell. His lips get really dry when he's hungry." Look at those clouds, Papa! They look like animals and people. That one over there is a caballo. That one over there looks like Mama, fat like Mama. It's a storm! "A little water, Raúl? Here, drink. Drink it down." No. Not near the river. It grows. On the edge, almost touching the water? He said no. The river grows. Tall? Tall. Like a palm tree? Taller than a palm tree. And everything is gone after that? Gone. And you die. Will the river kill us, Papa? No, Lito. It's far. The water won't reach us.

"You shouldn't have brought Andre and Paola. Children shouldn't be exposed to this kind of thing . . ." You lift the machete, high and far from your face. You strike low, very low, a clean blow, with strength. Like a man. With strength. There, you see. Away from your face. You finish it off with your hands. Pull it. Then peel it with your knife, down, down, down. See? It's all gone. You can eat it. Sweet, eh? That sugar cane is the sweetest we've had in years. "Take them outside, Genny. Play with them outside. But watch out for the cars. Those people next door drive through this place like they're going to tear it down. Crazy Americans. Go on. Outside." You're not afraid of anything, verdad, mijo? Not even of snakes? You've got to watch out for those. You be careful, ta bien? A snake can gobble down a little boy like you in one gulp. And it would get fat from having you inside its belly.

"Did he go this morning?" "No, he didn't." "That's probably why he's so restless. He must've gone in his diaper. "Pisspisspiss. Where does it go? In the water. No noise. How come? Chico, why is it so quiet? Pissing quiet. "Raúl! Stop that! You're going to make your hand bleed, old man!" The pain again. Like a knife in your guts. Goes down to your feet and then it's gone. The pain is gone, Papa! "You have to go there and make him stop. He won't do it all by himself. He can't control his hands, or his legs . . ." Need a wife. Big families in Santa Clara. Women. Strong women. Not pretty. A wife. Work here in the finca. Not pretty? Strong hands. Children. Boys. Many boys. "Raúl. Look, the dulce that you like. Gladys made it for you. Pudín. Like it? Good, ah? Made

88

by your daughter, Gladys. And they brought you Sara Lee. But that's for dessert. Rico, ah?" Chulita. You smell clean. Sebia, your sister smells clean, like you. Why isn't she fat like you, Sebia? "Abuelo, Abuelito. How are you doin', chico? You know who this is?" Look at you, Gordita. You've grown! Almost taller than me. Thank you Gordita. You're a kind soul, kinder than all those other people. "You're cute, you know that? You are c-u-t-e." Thank you, ah yes, on my eyes. It feels cool on my eyes. They burn so much, all the time. Cool. Your fat little hands are cool, Chulita.

"OK, Raúl. Time for your bath!" I told you, Raulito, I told you! Now you stand it. Next time you pay attention to what I say, mijo. Don't listen to that crazy guajiro that you have for a father. He thinks you're a man. And look at you, you're just a little boy, my muchachito. "He's like a mule this man! Come on Raúl, don't make me work so hard." Guajiro loco! Loco! Leave me alone. Don't push me! Don't touch me. Crazy guajiro, yes! Mama's right. You think you can tell me what to do. You think you can push me like a sack of boniato? Cabrón. Coño coño coño! Who are you, anyway? Sebia! Who is this man? Why is he hurting me? What is he doing to me, Sebia?! Tell him to go, por favor. Tell him to let me go, to let me be free.

Dear Peg,

How ya doin? Que pasa hombre? You should see my room! its so cool, radical, the narliest room you have ever seen! It has pictures of a whole bunch of people on my wall and door. It has pictures of big country, the police, michael jackson, billy idol, 4 of duran duran, and the poster you sent me of your band, that one is in the middle, I like the name of your band, how'd ya think of it, JULIAN AND THE L.A. SCENE. That's radical! What name did you have before, when you were doing stuff in Spanish? You didn't have a name did you? Just JULIAN, right? Or was it Julian y los Angelinos?

GENNY AND THE HAWTHORNE SCENE

The Best Home in Torrance

We need you, Nito.

Yes, Abuela. I know. I'm here.

It's difficult for us . . . without you . . .

How about getting some help?

The retirement home is out of the question.

But there are some good places.

He's violent. No place is going to take in a violent man. He'll hurt somebody. Look at my arms. Look at your father's arms. He'll grab you and won't let go. He's furious.

Maybe we could get a nurse, or someone to come in and help you with the house, the shopping, you know . . .

No. I don't want a stranger in my house.

Does he really get all that violent?

Yes. But he doesn't know it's us he's hurting.

The afternoon when she found me sitting outside, on the porch. That morning I had fallen down from my bike and had broken my left arm. She picked up one of the sheets of paper that I was using to write songs, and started to wipe off her tears with it. She cried, and looked at my arm in a cast. She cried, in despair, she touched my head. And cried for me. Today she thinks I'm going to poison myself with rotten food or catch some fatal disease or have a terrible accident on the road. Her grandson Julianito is a perfect target for assassins. One of these days, she's sure, I will be shot by demented fans. Fans!! And what about all the great singers of the past? What ever became of them? Who mentions them now? Who thinks of them? People today have lost their sense of beauty. They appear on television, Cubans too, from Miami, dressed in rags, wearing tennis shoes and blue jeans. Goodness, in Cuba not even the poorest of the poor in Zonalegre would appear in public dressed like that. Her grandson Julianito dresses like a pordiosero, a sad beggar. She didn't raise me and spend time cleaning my ass off so that I would repay her in this way: becoming another one of those unstable artists. Look at Johnny, he's younger than you and he already has a wife, a pretty wife from Colombia, two beautiful children, a boy and a girl; he bought a rich man's home in Torrance, goes to work in the morning, comes home in the evening and spends the weekends with the family. Look at Johnny, she says.

We're friends now. He loves my children. And he gets along just fine with Laura. They talk about music and literature. She likes all that junk. Yeah, I'm sure we're friends now. But it wasn't always that way. We never liked each other when we were growing up. We fought and beat each other up all the time. I know what he thinks. He thinks I'm a capitalist pig, a good for nothing Yuckie. A Young Upcoming Cuban Imbecile. But hell, all I want is a good home for my family. I've never done anything but work. Started at thirteen, in that restaurant on Hawthorne Boulevard, cleaning tables. Then I went to The Trade School in Carson City. Right after high school I got a real job, fixing TV sets. The boss was a son of a bitch, though. Papi wanted to go to the shop one day and set fire to the entire place. He said you get out of there, Johnny, that pig is exploiting you. And he sure was. I worked in factories after that, in machinery, fixing machines. And then here. I guess it's been about ten years. Junior Engineer first, when I didn't even have a B.S. Then I was put in charge of the entire Department of Product and Test Engineering. Schematics. Specifications. And $43,000 a year. Another one of the big shots at the International Testing Company, ITC. Old man Carl had had that job since the early days of the company. Lonely bachelor. I remember his dogs and his motorhome. Poor man. I came in and ten months later he got fired.

I work hard. But I've never traveled like Nito has. I haven't seen the world. I've taken trips with Laura and the kids to the mountains. We go to the Zoo. Some day I want to have a house in Palos Verdes. That's not materialism, shit, that's what any normal, decent human being in this country would aspire to. But Julian doesn't see things that way. He's not like the rest of us. He's never been like us. But he is a good man, Jul. He's here when he's needed, like now. He drops whatever he is doing and he jumps on a plane and there he is, ready to help. But then, he doesn't have a steady job and a home and a family. He's free.

First it was Abuelo Toledo; cancer of the bladder. Papi was young, very young, but he didn't leave his father's side. Then it was Abuela Josefa. Another case of cancer, in the stomach. I loved her so. It was such a joy to spend time with her, to chat about Spain, the early days of her life with Toledo. She encouraged me to continue working hard, doing whatever I wanted to do, to chase the dream, she would say: It is important to chase one's dreams. I'll never forgive myself for being away when she died. But Papi was with her. I know he comforted her.

Paco. Cabrón. He doesn't deserve for me to consider

93

him my brother. He would come to see her once a week. He would sit there and curse the entire time he was with her. One night he left the hospital room screaming, calling me this and that, saying that I had no right to make any demands on him. But I wasn't asking him for anything. I just sat there and I watched him. He knew what I was thinking. That son of a bitch. And you know what, Julián? You were the only one she called at the last minute. You were there, with her. This young man came to bathe her. He had curly hair like you and was wearing a green gown, like those shirts you wear sometimes. And my mother thought it was you. "Nito, muchacho!" she said. "What are you doing here?" But it's your grandfather that concerns me now. My mother's gone.

Abuelo, Tabaquito, you know who this is? Do you recognize me? It's me, Johnny, your grandson. Abuelo, look at me, look at my eyes. Remember when we'd go fishing? We'd get up real early in the morning, at five, and we would go to the Redondo Pier. Remember? We used to take long walks around the neighborhood looking for bottles. Remember Abuelo? We looked at the women and we talked about how beautiful they were. Huh? What's that? What are you saying? Speak up, Abuelo. I don't understand what you're saying. What about the women?

He calls me Gordita. I kneel in front of him and I kiss him. I comb his hair and fix his pillow. I also loosen his belt. Sometimes it's so tight he can hardly breathe. Then I talk to him. I tell him stories about school, my friends, the songs

I'm writing. I don't think he knows that I'm his granddaughter Geneia, but he listens, and he knows he's loved. One day I sat there by his feet and I took out my music magazines and just relaxed. I put one of my arms on his lap, and his hand, that big hand of his all of a sudden started moving very slowly towards my arm. It came down and softly, very softly, caressed me. He smiled. He called me in a whisper, Gordita. He seemed so happy to have me there, next to him.

The kids visit for a while and then they go on with their lives. But I have to face him day in day out. Juan and Gladys take us to the park once a week. It's not easy. We have to lift him and put him in his wheelchair and make sure that he's tied in well. He likes the sun. I like the air and the green grass and the sky. We're lucky if he doesn't throw one of his tantrums. There he is, one minute quiet and peaceful, the next minute he starts beating down on the arms of the chair with his fists, hard, hard, until he can no longer stand the pain. Sometimes he talks about Cuba. And he talks about the past. I get scared when that happens, because it's always his father and his brothers that he talks about. Dead people.

After the stroke he started singing. How strange, we thought. He had never sung before. And then he started rhyming. Everything he said, he said in a rhyme, like a Guajiro song, with farm-dance lyrics. He was in a great mood all the time. He didn't grump around complaining about this country and the gringos in the neighborhood, or about having to clean the driveway and take out the trash for the entire complex. He smiled and told jokes. Then one day Mima called me; she sounded upset. She said could I please run to help her. What happened? She was in tears. When I walked in the door I saw my father standing on top of the dining room table, playing with the lamp on the ceiling, saying you devil, why don't you stand still, can't you see that we want you to stand still?!

It wasn't easy to get him down, from there.

Not long after that Mima greeted me at the door with a desperate look on her face: "He's peeing all over the carpet!" she said. "I followed him with this bedpan, holding it under his thing, but he wouldn't use it. He wanted a corner, that one there, and that's where he did it. I feel exhausted, Gladys. I don't know what to do." "We'll get him diapers," said Juan. "Huge diapers." "Hah!" reacted Mima. "You'll never get him to wear those things. You don't realize who you're dealing with. Mister Hard Head. Never." We tried the diapers. At first he ripped them off. Then he forgot about them and started playing with the pictures on the walls and the million knick knacks Mima had in the house. That was fine, until he cut himself with a broken vase. The next phase was the saddest of all: He wanted to run, to leave the house. He said his father was waiting for him in the thickets, by the royal palms. He said he must hurry, or his father would leave without him. In the middle of the night, there he was, trying to get the door opened so he could run away.

We had no choice. We had to tie him up.

Abuela has been after Papi for a long time, asking him to write to Nito, to tell him that he has to come home. She says that if Nito were here things would be different. She would be happier and she would have more strength to deal with Grandpa. But Mami argues with Grandma. Mami says it's unfair to ask Nito to move back here. She argues with Papi, too. But he won't listen. And Grandma won't listen either. Whatever Papi or Grandma say is what gets done around here. Mami is very proud of Nito. She says that he has dreams, big dreams, and that he has worked hard to make a name for himself. She says I should be proud of him too. And I am. Of course I am. I tell all my friends at school about my Big Bro Nito, the famous singer and composer and performer and rock star. I show them the newspaper clippings he sends me. And I tell them that when I get a little older he'll let me sing with his band. And we'll write songs together. And he'll let me make records with him. He took me to a recording studio once and it was like maximum raging, man. You know, like in a movie. All these awesome synthesizers and the glass wall and the lights and the buttons and the microphones. And Nito put on those earphones like I thought he would and then he directed the band with his hands and showed the other guys how he wanted the music to go. Like in a movie, you know.

This was supposed to be the best home in Torrance. It was called City Gardens or Gardens something or other. Highly recommended. Expensive. So Juan, Nito and I went to see it. I thought, why not, maybe they would take better care of him in one of those places. From the outside it looked so nice: a small building surrounded by palm trees and flowers; then through a glass wall I saw the faces. Old people; some completely worn out; some in wheelchairs; some pierced by tubes of all sizes and colors. Sad faces pressed against the glass. The stink hit me the minute I walked in. An intense smell of urine and decay and cheap soup. The woman in charge of the nurses was friendly. She gave us a tour of the facilities. In the rooms, many of them were lying, face up, their eyes fixed on the ceiling; others were watching television. In the recreation room there was a young nurse singing and trying to get the old ones to sing with her. She greeted us and offered us a place to sit. But I couldn't stay. I just wanted to run, to shut my eyes and run.

Dear Pegasus,

How ya doin? Thanks for sending me the music maga-zine with your picture in it! I like what they say about your band, that you have a new sound, Caribbean rock, right? But it sounds more like techno-pop to me. They say that L.A. SCENE has a nice blend of Latin and American. Well, that's who we are! I like the story about The Police. That dude Sting is radical man! (I WANT MY MTV!!) Are you planning to make a video? Tell your agent that you want to make one and Can I be in it please?! Pretty please?!

You know I'm really dressing radical now. I'm keeping my grades up I think! Say hi to Erica for me. She's so cool. I miss ya . . . I love ya . . .

Rad Unicorn

STEP THREE

Crazy Love

In the key of Bb minor. Simple chords. Simple and beautiful. So much beauty in simplicity. All his melodies had a similar cadence. The heart rending legato, the crescendos. And a baby voice that suddenly exploded in the last note, pushing forward, upward, to the sky. The Women. Always present. A choir of angels. Now how can we get that faraway feeling across, you know, that feeling of Eden. The strumming. Very typical fifties. It changes now. *Everything's wrong.* It becomes sadder. You're doomed from the moment you find this crazy love. *Heaven above.* Can you call for help? Heaven? Hello, hello! Calling Heaven. Hello? Is anybody there? Can that powerful Heaven really set you free?

Three times *Don't.* There's feeling there. Begging, kneeling in front of your oppressor and asking for mercy. *Don't don't don't you see/ What you are doing to me?* I hold the mike with my left hand (A very young Sinatra?), lean forward, my right hand reaching out and pointing to an imaginary lover in the crowd, an invisible object of desire. Or perhaps the hand is defying that queen of your nightmares, the ever-present ever-tempting Island. Or slapping the face of an old woman, striking the nose of a nineteen-year-old father. *Can't you see what you all did to me?*

Very straight now. *You upset my heart from the start.* Look back at the band. Hold that note. *Staaaart.* Low, long, languid. Then pause and let it all be silent. One more time. This is it. *With your crazy love.* The same rocking chair melody, the same cradle. They were all so young, so very young then. Her dreamy eyes must've been open wide in those days, from the excitement, all the rules that she had to keep in mind, the surprise at the way people treated her, like a grown-up . . . I got married because I couldn't stand her anymore. She wouldn't let me do anything. No parties, no friends.

Couldn't even go to school because what good is school for a little girl, anyway. Women didn't need school. And when I got married, she meddled in everything your father and I did. She cooked for us and went on vacation with us and then when you were born she said she had to raise you because I didn't know how. Your father, with the temper he has, he's put up with a lot, more than most men would put up with. She accuses him of not taking good care of the family. How could he let me drive that car in the condition it's in. How could he let Geneia go to her graduation party alone, without one of us to chaperone her. She says I like "the street" too much. Can you believe that? I haven't even gone to San Diego. I haven't taken a plane since the day we arrived here from Cuba. And she has the nerve to say I like the street! May God forgive me for saying what I'm about to say, but, you know, she's paying for all the things she did to Pipo. Yes, I know he's never been one to take control of things, but it wasn't fair for her to leave him alone for days, eating junk because she had to come to my house and do my chores or go traveling with me and your father. Left him alone because she thought I wouldn't know how to raise a family. And now look at her. She's stuck with him. She continues to meddle in my affairs; she wants to run my life. But she's stuck with him . . .

The same swing, this version of "Crazy Love," same thing except . . . The Latin Crossover, that's what it is. The get down part. When the group becomes one voice, and it's the voice and the congas, the cymbals, the palito, and we make this crazy love sound, like Salsa, Mozambique, Merengue, Cha cha chá, Mambo, Samba, Rumba, Calypso, Bembé. The brass, good, blow it, yeah, give it to me, that brass. The bass. And I've added strings, five, six violins flowing, can't you hear them? Pizzicato. You sing, loud, like you're gonna fart, supporting with your ass what is almost ready to come out of your mouth. I lower my body, bend my knees again, hold the mike close to my mouth. Then I come up, bringing from the lowest of lows that crisp *Craaaaaaaaa* one octave down *zyyyyyy*. And now my lungs, my abdomen, my asshole, my throat, my mouth support the last boisterous, hurtful, desperate cry in crescendo. Hold it. *Looooooooooooooooooooove*. Yeah, my version is the same, except.

I'm sweating, my knees are shaking, I feel exhausted, clean, fulfilled, not hungry, not thirsty, not nervous, not afraid, much calmer, the happiest I have ever felt. How much longer will they hold that applause? Relax. You've kept your end of the deal. They will listen to you on smoggy L.A. afternoons. You will live in the grooves that speak for you and through you. Relax. Too late to return to Zonalegre, to Varadero, to Gardena, to Leuzinger High, to El Camino College, to the Island. You've broken away. This is freedom. Everything else is painful, empty, repetitive . . . She says she doesn't understand why our family can never be happy. She talks about happiness! But you can't expect happiness to fall from Heaven. You have to work for it and make yourself deserving of it. What she really means is that this family doesn't fit into her mold, into her idea of what a family should be. Why won't she let go of the past? Why can't she realize that we're far, so far from Cuba? Does one need to be born again, with a different brain, in order to understand something as simple as that?

Listen, listen to the clapping, and the angels in the back, giggling and flapping their wings, dropping feathers all over the floor, and your own voice inside your head, saying, "You did it." If you can remember this moment, then everything you do from now on will make sense. Remember it. And add to it another moment, weaving your life. An ongoing melody. All of it written by you . . . No, it doesn't help to explain things calmly to her, to be logical and patient. She'll promise you the world. Yes, she'll say that she understands, that she will try to change. And five minutes later she'll ask me if I put gas in the car, or she'll scold me for not calling her before I went to run an errand, or she'll criticize me for not giving Geneia the "right" advice about the future (she doesn't want Geneia to go off to college some day), or for not spending enough time at home. She runs after me, imploring me not to go to the mall because there are gangs in the mall, didn't I know that? Why did I turn out so irresponsible and feisty!

So relax now, OK? Be yourself. Put your hand on your hip or on your shoulder if you feel like it, cross your legs, go on, they won't beat you up for it, they love you. All right, that's it. Now extend your arms, far, there you go, lower your head, you draw in your arms, crossed, your hands touching your chin. Up again, smiling wide. Ample Julian Smile. Such a pretty boy, posing on the Roman scene, the famous Spanish steps in Rome with his manager Irvin Feld. "Diana," he wrote it at the age of fifteen and it sold more than four million copies internationally. On the back cover of the Golden Album. Ah yes. "While his success has already been unusual, I believe that what has gone before is merely a preface. Paul's talents are now beginning to ripen and his message as composer-singer gets richer. One day it will come into full force and its impact will be fantastic." Coñó! ITS IMPACT WILL BE FANTASTIC. La nota final: "Creating and singing songs is one thing Paul *must* do." Yes? That's why you should relax, be yourself. You must do it, yes. Under the spotlight, right in the center, in front, this is where I need to be. In full force. Fantastic.

Hi Nito, how you doin dude? How bout Erica? Is she still cool as I left her last? Give her an elephant kiss and hug for me, OK? Liked the t-shirts I sent you? Ones for u, Big J, and 1 is 4 Special E. (Kool Knicknames!) The blue 1 is for u and the white 1 is for Special E.

Well this is it for now, Hasta la vista, I LOVE U

Yours truly,

Tricky in California

A Broken *Home*

Geneia is sitting on the bed, next to Julian. She listens. Gladys picks up the clean laundry and starts folding the socks and the underwear. She listens. Nito wants to say more. But he's said so much already. He's said enough.

I put my life into boxes and I run here thinking, coño, how great, I'm going to see Mami again, and my Genny. Then . . .

It won't help, Gladys tells herself once again. It won't help to cry and to get emotional.

Then what?

This house crushes me.

What's so bad about this house?

Everything.

She's heard her brother talk like that before. He hates Papi. She doesn't really know why. Abuela hates him too. That time when she picked up the phone and heard Nito's voice and Abuela's. They were talking about Papi. But she loves her Daddy. She loves him so . . . Oh yeah, she remembers now, there was that other time when she couldn't stand it anymore and she told Nito to shut up and stop saying bad things about her Daddy.

You can't expect to find everything nice and perfect all the time. That's not normal. No home is perfect. There are always problems . . .

Yes. Abuelo and Abuela need you. Now. But what about before? What about all those times when you wanted to have your friends over and he'd say no, that you couldn't? Or people from work came over to visit you, to see your plants or your furniture or whatever, and he'd scream Coño all over the place?

It's not my right to make decisions in this house . . .

He thinks you're stupid . . . And then there's Abuela.

She's just like him. That's why they never got along. Two power-thirsty monsters.

Should she say something now? He's calling her Daddy a monster. That's not right. No son should call his father a monster. She loved Nito so much. He was like her second daddy. No. The other Daddy. Because she had two fathers, one who was Cuban and one who was American, or almost American. The old father and the young one. She could talk to Nito about her fears and her nightmares and her fantasies. He understood her. She could talk to Papi about other important things. But now Nito was saying that her daddy was a monster. She had to do something. Didn't she?

Big Bro, don't say things like that, please.

Genny, I'm sorry.

Go outside, Genny. You shouldn't be listening to all this.

No, Mami. Let her stay . . .

They wanted to watch a movie on the VCR, so they went to Hawthorne Videos and looked at what seemed to Julian like half a million titles and descriptions. "It's all the same trash," he told her. "Nothing good here." "But look," she was holding two video boxes. "You'll like these. I swear." "*War Games* and *Dream Scape*. Why do you think I'll like them?" " 'Cause . . . that one is like science fiction. And Matthew Broderick is so cute, you'll like him. The other one is about dreaming. You talk about dreams. You tell me your dreams all the time. You'll like that one." So they rented the two films. "How strange," Geneia told Julian the next day. "We had our own war games, in the house, right here. Our own war games."

That Saturday morning, at around ten, Gladys' cousin Luis had come to visit. Luis was also her godson. She loved him. Luis had quite a story to tell and he hadn't gotten it out of his system yet. "We were in Panama, you know. We got this little house and made friends with the neighbors. We waited. Our relatives here in the North were helping us. They sent us money. I got a job as a mechanic, my trade. And we waited. One day we decided we couldn't wait anymore. I told Cari, look, Cari, we are going to get to the North, no matter what. So we traveled to Mexico, Tijuana. And these people, a married couple, they were kind and offered to help. Cuban people. They took the children. They would pretend to be their parents. And us, well, Cari hid inside this tiny ice box, and I hid under one of the beds, in the back of the trailer, you know. And then, well, they stopped us. They interrogated Luisita, they made her cry, and Tony, such a little boy, he cried from the moment he saw the police. But we made it. When Cari got out of the ice box she couldn't walk. I was all right. The kids had nightmares for a long time. But we're here. We made it."

Gladys had heard the story many times. This morning, at around eleven, they were talking about the other relatives who still remained in Cuba. She made coffee for him and they sat on the couch, in the living room, and they laughed. They remembered the mischievous things they did when they were young, in Santa Clara, when he was eight and she just a couple of years older. They liked to talk about Tía Luca, about Tío Marcos, and about Frances, his crazy sister from Las Vegas, the one who went berserk and started dancing in night clubs. "She's a good sister," he'd always say, not hiding his shame very well, "crazy but good. She helped us a lot when we were in Panama." Gladys loved Luis. And she was glad that he had managed to leave; glad that she had his company again, his laughter and his memories.

That morning, at around eleven, Juan walked into the house. He passed by the living room and headed for the kitchen. He grabbed a cup, opened the thermos and served himself some coffee. Then he went to his room. He slammed the door and didn't open it until approximately four that afternoon. Almost an entire day, Gladys thought, locked up in there. He's doing it again. He's back to his old ways. But no, she reconsidered. He wasn't "back." He was always that way. He had good days, a few each month. Getting that door slammed in her face was the norm.

He came out and told her that he wasn't going to have dinner. Oh yes, because that was the punishment. Whenever he got pissed he didn't eat her food. Then he sat in the living room and watched TV for an hour. Genny sat next to him. She had stayed away, in her world, with her songs and her magazines and her telephone calls most of the day. But dinner time was approaching. She wanted him to be there. "You're going to eat with us, Papi?" "No, you go ahead. I'm not hungry." "But you gotta eat, Papi. Come on." "No, mija. Not tonight." "All right." At approximately five-fifteen Juan got up. He went to his room and slammed the door again. "What's with him?" asked Julian. "The same old thing. He's upset because Luis came to visit. He doesn't like for people to visit me, you know, not even my godson." Julian felt the blood rush to his head. An ocean of blood. "He's crazy. That man is crazy." She put her index finger over her lips, asking him to keep silent. "No use," she said. "He'll never change."

Dinner was served at six, a few minutes after Julian and Geneia had arrived from the video store. Gladys and her children sat at the table and started to eat, quietly. Then he came out, dragging the mattress. He dropped it on the floor of the recreation room, which was just a few steps away from the table where his family sat, eating. "Cabrona!" he screamed, "you have no right! No right!" His closed fists hit the walls.

He paced up and down the room, around the table. "Ca-brona!" Juan stopped a few feet away from Gladys. "Ca-brona!" Julian couldn't wait any longer. "You hit Mami and I'm going to beat the shit out of you!" He stood so close to his father he could smell his breath and feel the heat of his body. Juan pushed him. "This is none of your business!" "She is my business!" Juan collapsed on the mattress. He was shaking. Geneia covered him with her arms. He suddenly seemed frail and afraid. "Cálmate, Papi, please," she whispered in his ear. "Calm down, Papito. You shouldn't get like this, look at you, you're trembling, Papi . . ."

We had our own war games. Didn't we, Nito?

There should be some kind of a screening machine that checks for people like him, that finds the rotten ones and throws them onto a pile. Rejects. It's easy to go and get married and have children, but then what? Here's the mold they used with us and you're going to have to fit into it. That's the only way, right? Fit in there or die.

We were young, Nito. We didn't know any better.

But what about Abuela? She wasn't that young.

For Mami the world is black and white, Heaven and Hell, angels and demons . . .

Cubans and Americans . . . She should've never left Cuba.

You're cruel.

No. Take a plant or a fruit tree that only grows in the tropics and plant it in a cold land. It will die, or go crazy, turn poisonous.

She's terrified. This world is too big and too threatening for her.

She should've stayed in her casita, with her people. She should've never left.

She says the same thing about the family, that we should've never come to this country.

Why do you take it all so quietly? You never raise your voice. Never talk back. Aren't you fed up?

Yes, I am. But there's nothing I can do about it. Not now.

It's never too late. I'll help you.

What about Genny? She will suffer . . .

She will suffer more if you stay with him.

It would be too painful for my little girl.

She would be happier in the long run, I assure you.

She loves her father, Nito.

She'll continue to see him.

On weekends . . . A broken home. How sad.

Dear Julian,

HI!! How are you doing? I'm fine here. I got GREAT grades on my report. Three A's!! Only two C's. What do you think?

Let's talk about MIGUEL BOSE! Thank you for sending me his music; he's really cute. Those Spaniards are really happening, can't believe it. Cause some of the Mexican singers on SIB look victimized, totally victimized. Is Miguel Bosé as raging in person as he is on the record? Maximum raging! I have a problem with him sometimes, cause I can't understand what he's saying. Not because it's in Spanish, because you know I understand Cuban Spanish pretty well. It's his accent, Castellean, right?

You know, the music in English now SUCKS! There are a few exceptions. The band YOUNG MEN EATING MEN is one of them. I also like the songs from the 50's and 60's. Guess what? I'm head artist of the classroom. I think I'm gonna follow in your footsteps! As an artist. As you see in the newspaper, I did a comic strip. It's called "Sorry, Charlie." I didn't like it and neither did my readers. I got a new one out, which I think will be a success. It's called "Alien Rock." Every month I'll send you a copy of the paper.

You won't believe how big Andie is getting. He comes over and destroys everything in his way. And Paola helps him too you know. She's so tiny, though, in comparison. She's learning how to talk and she walks already! I can't wait for you to see them. I love those children so much!

I've written songs. The titles of my latest songs are "COME FOLLOW ME," "ALWAYS SEE THE LIGHT," "NEW GENERATION," "LITTLE ANGEL," "HAPPILY EVER AFTER," AND "THE WOMAN." As soon as I get a chance to work on them a little more I'll send them to you. If you like them, maybe you could record them with your band.

Love you lots,

Geneia

A *Party* Band

JULIAN: And there's Joe the Macho. When we get down sabrosón, tú sabe, that's when Joe really happens, don't you think? When he's allowed to play the güira and the timbales and the maracas and the congas . . .

LUCHO: I couldn't care less.

JULIAN: Lucho: What a natural, eh? When he jammed with us the first time, he played his drums like he was making love to them, passionate and thundering love . . . Remember?

ROLI: No, I don't.

JOE: What the hell does "thundering love" sound like?

JULIAN: And then he picked up Joe's guitar and there he went, like he was born playing it. And then he came to me and he said, "Would you let me play your organ?"

LUCHO: And you let me . . .

ROLI: Chuckle Chuckle.

JULIAN: Picture this. A few days later . . .

JOE: There they go again. Shit!

ROLI: Shut up, Joe!

JULIAN: A glimpse of their legs on the bed. Seductive music . . .

LUCHO: "You're so vain . . . You probably think this song is about you . . ."

JULIAN: The torsos reflected on a mirror that's on the wall, above the bed, both flowing in energy and power; the hands caress the bodies, almost full bodies now, the necks, long and curved, the faces, youthful, perspiring. The faces smile, pleased . . .

JOE: Faggots!

LUCHO: And many years later . . .

JULIAN: The four of us and Erica in concert . . .

LUCHO: Erica and her Cuban peeps.

JULIAN: Look at her: ethereal and beautiful. To her left, on keyboards, is Julian, dressed in black, rugged, thunderdomish . . .

LUCHO: Thunderwhat?!

JULIAN: To my right is Lucho, on drums, his Cheshire cat smile is inviting . . .

LUCHO: Meow.

JULIAN: Then Roli and Joe, on guitars, virile, explosive, suggestive.

JOE: Y-e-a-h!

JULIAN: Picture a Hollywood bash, lots of gays, punks . . .

JOE: Shit!

JULIAN: And an assortment of Bananarama-Go-Go-Bangle types. Julian is standing by the entrance door, next to an Andy Warhol or a Picasso. He's dressed casually: jeans and black T-shirt; he's wearing brown-tinted sunglasses . . .

JOE: You think you look so c-o-o-l with those glasses, don't you? I bet you wear them even when you take a crap.

LUCHO: Julian, am I there, with you, in that Hollywood bash?

JULIAN: Of course. You're sitting on a couch, a few feet away from me . . . Suddenly, Erica walks in the door . . .

LUCHO: Fuck!

JULIAN: She seems futuristic: dress, makeup, hairdo, pose, eyes, everything in her belongs to another era, distant, unknown. As she moves, she looks back at Julian, whose eyes are already fixed on her.

ROLI: I thought you said you met in New York . . .

JULIAN: Yes, this fateful encounter between Leading Man Julian and his ingeniously *Outre* could have also taken place in New York, yes, when both the Cuban American pianist . . .

ROLI: Bravo! Viva el Maestro!

JULIAN: . . . and the Kansan Mennonite-Turned-Ericamor crossed each other's path at the Museum of Art, where the Salsero Julianito wrote "Guernica In New York."

LUCHO: The song that will make him go down in history.

ROLI: Or so they say.

JOE: Goooood weed.

LUCHO: Listen to this . . .

JULIAN: What is it?

LUCHO: *I, Tina.*

JOE: Do we have to . . .

ROLI: Shut up, Joe!

LUCHO: You'll like this part. Listen: "Julian began to look upon Little Erica as his ticket, at last, out of West Hawthorne. He lusted for the New Wave big time—the Apollo in New York, the Howard Theatre in Washington, D.C., the Regal in Chicago . . ."

JULIAN: Lust for the Big Time, yes.

LUCHO: "But Julian and the L.A. Scene—as sharp and exciting as they were—were still essentially a party band: capable of covering any hit, but short of original material . . ."

JULIAN: History repeats itself.

ROLI: Except that you're not into wife beating and there's no one around here who could measure up to Tina.

JOE: That Mamota is hot.

JULIAN: I sure can relate to her. I know how it feels to be fearing that blow that can come down on your face at any minute, for the stupidest reasons, that iron fist that crushes you like your head is a rotten egg . . .

LUCHO: Julian is still afraid of his father.

JULIAN: And you, Lucho, are still afraid of God.

JOE: I thought we were talking about Tina here.

ROLI: "You must understand that the touch of your hand makes my pulse react . . ."

LUCHO: Pow!

JOE: On the nose.

LUCHO: Pow!

JOE: On the mouth.

LUCHO: Pow!

JOE: On the jaw.

ROLI: "What's love got to do, got to do with it . . ."

JULIAN: So, anyway, what makes us so different from all the other groups?

ROLI: We don't do drugs.

JULIAN: We sure do.

JOE: You call this drugs? This insignificant roach?

JULIAN: We're a very boring and ordinary bunch, aren't we?

LUCHO: Except that we're Cuban.

JOE: That makes us loud.

JULIAN: Melancholy.

ROLI: That makes us e-x-o-t-i-c.

JULIAN: Traitors to our brothers here.

ROLI: Traitors to our brothers there.

LUCHO: Politically incorrect.

JULIAN: That's right, viejo, no matter where we stand . . .

JOE: H-e-a-v-y!

ROLI: Listen to this, it's from *The Rolling Stone* . . .

JOE: Again?!

ROLI: Shut up, Joe! "SHOCK. How else could one respond to the revelation that Boy George was now addicted to heroin? . . ."

LUCHO: The two heroines together at last!

ROLI: "It's well known that George is homosexual . . ."

JULIAN: No! Really?

ROLI: "George is very much a sponge; he absorbs people's personalities . . ."

JULIAN: How about some atmosphere?

ROLI: "The apartment was painted in pastels—pale peach and pink—and photo-realist paintings of Marilyn Monroe, Elvis and James Dean, as well as an immense collage of Madonna, decorated the walls. There was a jacuzzi in George's marble bathroom and, of course, video equipment and a stereo in the enormous living room. A box of marijuana sat on the coffee table . . ."

JULIAN: Roli was really talking about himself there, wasn't he? Reading about George but he really meant *Roli.*

LUCHO: Like, it's well known that he's a homosexual . . .

JULIAN: But not *just* a homosexual, he's also a sponge, isn't he? He absorbs people's personalities.

LUCHO: And nationalities, a common problem with some of us young Cubans.

ROLI: Don't pick on me today, please.

JULIAN: And that apartment with the pink and Marilyn and James Dean and all that, you're picturing Roli's apartment, don't you think?

ROLI: I don't have pink walls!

JULIAN: The way those Cuban women in Miami go crazy over Roli . . .

JOE: What a joke.

JULIAN: The way they salivate over his . . . his charm . . .

LUCHO: He's so C-U-B-A-N-O.

JULIAN: So mahssculeeene!

JOE: So Más-Culón.

LUCHO: Why, Joe, he doesn't look like a woman at all! If he were more effeminate then maybe . . .

JOE: You guys fuck each other all you want. I don't care. But leave me out of it.

JULIAN: Do you ever wonder what people think of us, how they see us?

LUCHO: Our "fans" you mean? If they only knew that we've all been tested for AIDS . . .

ROLI: And that we continue to have orgies once in a while . . .

JOE: Not with me you don't.

LUCHO: Of course not.

ROLI: Joe is the exception.

JULIAN: He's not into decadence.

LUCHO: He's just afraid that he might like it too much.

JOE: Rrrr!!

JULIAN: Finally! A confrontation!

ROLI: Just jabbering and nothing happening. No conflicts. No fatal illnesses, no death beds . . . Finally . . .

JULIAN: All right, Joe. Enough! Leave Lucho alone.

JOE: !!!!

LUCHO: See . . . See what . . . I . . . mean? He's a closet sadist! Cabrón!

ROLI: How about doing a song from our first album.

JULIAN: What an orchestra we had for that one!

ROLI: Violins and a harp and four pretty madrileñas going ba-duh-duhhh . . . How about the second album?

JULIAN: Much too engagé for this party . . . Let's do one from our best-seller.

LUCHO: We can't. Erica's not here. She did all the vocals.

JULIAN: Except for "Crazy Love." Yours truly did that one.

JOE: Where's Erica anyway?

JULIAN: I told her to take a hike for the day.

LUCHO: Uy! What a man! Let's do the oldie then.

JULIAN: A capella first. Craaazy Loooove . . . Nah!
Forget it.

LUCHO: What's the matter with you?

JULIAN: Don't you people get sick of it? Haven't you
made enough music already?

ROLI: Oh-oh. Are we getting heavy now, Julian?
Is this the part where you get philosophical and we crank up
the CD?

JULIAN: No, really, think about it. Think about all the
music we've played . . .

JOE: Un cojonal.

LUCHO: Everything except country.

JULIAN: Mellow. Hard. The Cuban Quinceañeras.
Even songs from Julio Iglesias' *América* . . .

LUCHO: "Guantanamera," "Recuerdos de Ypacaraí,"
"Júrame."

ROLI: Good old July Churches . . .

JULIAN: Don't you get sick of it sometimes?

JOE: No.

JULIAN: Now we're going American. What's the
name they've given this new thing we're doing?

JOE: Post-punk-post-new-wave-post-disco . . .

ROLI: Post-country-post-rapping-post-post-
post-Beatles . . .

LUCHO: Post-Elvis-post-Simon-and-Garfunkel-post-
Billy-Idol-post-British-Invasion-post-Cyndi-Lauper-post-
Blues-post-Soul-post-Michael-Jackson-post-Hustle-post-
Donna-Summer-post-Gloria-Gaynor-post-Prince-post-
Madonna . . .

JULIAN: Post-Bruce-post-Lionel-post-The-Supremes-
post-Diana-post-Tina-post-Dylan-post-We-Are-The-World-
We-Are-The-Children . . .

JOE: We're post-something, that's for sure.

LUCHO: And all thanks to Julian, who sacrificed his ass for fame.

JOE: Julian the Víctima.

JULIAN: Speak of the devil, did you ever read this?

JOE: *Amadeus*? Are you crazy?!

ROLI: Shut up, Joe!

JULIAN: You're gonna love this . . . "After a night of carousing, Julian comes home to find Lucho has cleared out, taking his drum set with him . . ."

LUCHO: Every single tamborcito, yes.

JULIAN: "Later, in mid-performance of 'Guantanamera,' Julian faints at the keyboard and is taken home by Lee-the-Manager-Agent who, realizing that they are alone, seizes this moment to carry out his devilish scheme . . ."

ROLI: The man has such a big . . . heart.

LUCHO: You should know.

JULIAN: "Suddenly the remorseful Lucho returns home, aghast to find his lover alone with his avowed enemy. To Lee's anguish, he locks Julian in his bedroom and sends Lee packing with: 'He's not to do this kind of thing anymore; it's making him ill.' "

ROLI: Yes, but what a way to go!

LUCHO: Has anybody ever seen a hornier bitch?

JULIAN: "Although Lee is once more frustrated in his war against the almighty Lucho, his urging of Julian to finish off what they had started before the jealous lover arrived drives the exhausted Cuban composer to an early grave . . ."

ROLI: Lee did help us out at the beginning.

JULIAN: Bah! He made promises that he never kept.

ROLI: He did take us around the country.

JOE: Stinking holes in Union City where fat Cuban mamas bounced around to our boleros and our Salsa.

ROLI: Flowers for the pigs.

JULIAN: Speak for yourself. Resentido!

LUCHO: Let's be fair with the man. He did take us to some fancy places.

ROLI: The Embassy, the Regency, the Tropique.

LUCHO: He did produce our first album.

JOE: He did know people in the business.

JULIAN: But if it hadn't been for Erica.

LUCHO: I'm gonna go rent a movie, man, this is getting boring.

JULIAN: No, Lucho. I won't talk about Erica anymore. I promise.

LUCHO: It has nothing to do with Erica. You're sick of music, right? Well, I'm sick of you.

JULIAN: Come back, please.

LUCHO: And do what? Get stoned? Bullshit our lives away?

JOE: Another filósofo!

JULIAN: You wanted fame, no? Well, now enjoy it, God damn it!

ROLI: Erica helped us a lot, yes, but she's also made changes . . .

LUCHO: Drastic changes.

JOE: So we have a new sound. What's wrong with that?

LUCHO: We have money now, that's all you care about.

JOE: I care about our work too, you fucking faggot.

LUCHO: You're a disgusting conguero. What do you know about music?!

JOE: Julian won't screw your ass anymore, eh? Isn't that it? Isn't that why you're so pissed off at Erica?

LUCHO: Can't you see that she's using us, Joe?

JOE: Bah! She would've made it without us . . .

LUCHO: Why do you let her do your job, Julian?

JULIAN: My job is to write and play music.

LUCHO: You don't care that we don't sound . . . Cuban anymore?

JULIAN: What's that supposed to mean anyway, "Cuban"?

LUCHO: Having another one of your patriotic crises, Julianito? . . . However you define it, Erica doesn't fit the definition.

JULIAN: Lucho, please, don't go . . .

Dear Nito and Erica,

Here's one of my songs. I wrote it for Andie. What do you think? Wanna write the music for it?

ALWAYS SEE THE LIGHT
(by Geneia Toledo)

Don't listen to the ones who say
I'm wrong
Just listen to
Oh listen to my song
It speaks of love
With love you'll always see the light

When you go to sleep
afraid of night
Just think of you and me
Look to the sky
You'll see us in the light
With love you'll always see the light

They may take you away from me
They say I'm not teaching you right
But I love you Baby Andre
and that will always be
as long as you can sing
this song
It speaks of love

my love
It brings you closer to the light

Go to sleep now
I'm by your side
Don't fear the night
my baby Andre
Look here
You see?
A tiny
loving
flickering light

All We *Need*

Is she all right now?

Yes, she's fine, but she cries at night and when you touch her tummy she says booboo, Papi, booboo.

Poor baby. She's so good-natured.

In comparison to Andre she's an angel.

But Andre's such a Toledo.

She's more like her mom. You know, nice and quiet and normal. The Toledos are so weird . . .

So you admit that you're kind of weird, too?

No jodas, Julian. I'm not admitting nothing. I'm just saying, my son takes after Papi, and his father, and his father's father. If you want the truth, well . . .

I know, you're the most normal of us all.

Maybe not the most normal, but the most settled, yes. Look at Paquito, he's into drugs, coke, and hanging out with an older woman, a Marielita from Miami. And Manolín, still making plastic shoes in New Jersey and spreading the word . . .

Like you used to.

I'm sure Jehovah thanked me when I dropped out of his gang.

No kidding! . . . I can't believe you changed so fast. You used to . . . Well, you were such a . . . you were so much like them.

Laura told me from the very beginning, she said, you want to be a Jehovah's Witness? Fine, so be it, but forget about marrying me. Her family's very Catholic, you know. When her father found out that his baby was marrying a Cubano he immediately asked for two things: a picture of me and a church wedding. He wanted the picture so he could make sure I wasn't black.

That's right. In Bogotá they think that anyone from the

Caribbean has to be black.

Yeah. He wanted to make sure that I wasn't negrito or mulato . . . and then he wanted to know if I was Catholic. White and Catholic, that's all he asked for.

Didn't he try to get your birth certificate or some document out of Cuba so you could be married in the Church?

The man's got clout. Can you imagine? He tried and he got it. Out of Cuba!

So you, the young minister of the Kingdom Hall, the knower of Truth, returned, thanks to Love, to your Catholic roots.

They bugged me for a long time. They would come asking for me and Laura would slam the door in their faces. He doesn't want to see you people, she'd tell them. Then they went to see me at work.

What did you tell them?

That I was married now and that I wanted to have children and that, if my children needed blood during an operation, I felt they should have it, that I would personally donate it. That's all. They went on and on and showed me the scriptures, as if I didn't know what they were quoting, as if I hadn't read them a million times. Then I said, look, those are words, if you want to believe in them, fine, that's your problem, but life, marriage, children, they're not made up of words . . .

Or not just words, anyway.

They stopped bugging me after a while.

Gave up on you, huh, John?

If Paola had needed blood for this operation and I had still been a Witness, there would've been a big problem.

Laura wouldn't have married you in the first place. So you wouldn't have had that dilemma.

I'd be lonely and miserable the way I was before I met her.

I'm glad it's working out for you, Johnny.

And what about you, when are you taking the bait?

Huh?

Marriage.

No. Not me.

But you live with Erica, don't you?

So?

Come on, Jul, what difference would it make? Do it for Abuela, she'd be so happy.

Can't.

What if you have children?

They're not in the picture . . . yet.

Don't you want 'em?

Some day.

You're getting old, Big Bro. Can't wait forever.

I'll have my children when I'm fifty, how about that?

Yeah, you'll be the father and grandfather all in one.

Does she still have the stitches?

Yes. For a few more days. You know, Jul, when they took her into the operating room I felt like they were tearing my heart out. You've got to be a father to understand that feeling. Like you're dying inside. Laura was crying. We couldn't even talk. Later she told me she was thinking she wasn't going to see her baby again. Hell, Bro, that was exactly what was going through my head . . . How long you gonna be around?

Who knows. I suppose . . . until the problem with Abuelo . . . gets resolved.

If what you mean is until he dies, you're gonna be with us for a long time. The old man is like a rock. If it weren't for his brain . . .

I'm not here waiting for him to die.

What do you mean, then?

I came to help in any way I can, you know . . .

Moral support is what they need.

I'm living next door, in one of the apartments.

For real?

But at one point or another I'm gonna have to split.

Bah, the band can get along without you.

Exactly.

The kids remember you a lot.

They hardly ever see me!

But they remember you. Laura plays your records and she shows them your pictures. Laura likes you. She wants them to remember you.

Ooooh, that's dangerous . . . They might hear a calling . . .

Shit, if one of my children turned into a crazy artist like you or my mother-in-law, I swear I would die. That's all we need. Another artist in the family.

How's Mariana doing?

Bad. Really bad.

What do you mean?

She's hurting for money. She started doing watercolors, to sell, and that didn't do it. So now, you're not gonna believe this, now she's cleaning houses!

Doesn't she get any help from her husband?

What? Are you out of your mind? She's worse than dirt as far as he's concerned.

What's their story?

Their marriage was arranged by their parents. He was twenty years older than her and he wanted her to be a typical wife. And she turned out to be an artist! Poor man.

So what happened?

When she decided that she wanted to have a career, he said no, and she said the hell with you, you old fart. And she left him.

Who kept the children?

He did. He hired a whole bunch of maids to take care of them. Mariana saw them once in a while . . .

Mariana's work is good, you know.

But artists always end up like that.

Fucking materialist society.

Rules of the game, Julián. No one makes a living from art. Unless you're famous.

I'm not cleaning houses.

But you've got a band and you play in night clubs and you've made records . . .

I've been lucky, I guess.

Lucky and smart, in spite of all your locura.

What do you mean?

Well, you were doing your Spanish thing at first, right?

Yes . . .

Then you realized that there was a bigger market out there and you started writing more commercial stuff, in English, so people, the American people, would buy your records, no?

Uh-huh.

And when you do your . . . your jigs . . .

Gigs.

When you do your gigs, you play all kinds of music, the popular junk too, don't you, the top ten?

Right.

You're smart.

No. I'm just a whore.

That, too.

Bueno, let's see, tell your tío where it hurts . . . There? Okay, show me. Aw, that's nothing, just a scratch. *He was leaving for San Francisco with the band. Five shows a week. Good money. Plenty of free time to write songs for an album. She called him three days before his trip. The doctor says I've got to have surgery. I'm losing too much blood. They're going to clean me out, Nito. And I'm scared. He tried to calm her down.* Does anybody know what I have here for my little Paola . . . something she likes . . . Can she guess what it is? *He told her it was a very common operation. Many women had it. Will you come and be with me? Of course, Mami. I'll be with you until you get better. Qué bueno, mijo, I don't think I could pull through without you. Mami, he laughed, you make it sound like I'm the doctor here. My doctor corazón, yes, you are.* Yes, mi amor, this is for you. Can you get up? No? It hurts too much? All right, how about if I lift you? You wanna take a little walk with Tío Julián? *He found her asleep, so calm and relaxed. It had gone fine, no complications. But they had to take a lot of crap out, the doctor told them. It was a mess in there. She shouldn't have waited this long. A tumor the size of an orange rotting inside of her for years. Why did she wait until now? He didn't even try to explain it to the young doctor. Will she be okay?, that's all he wanted to know. Yes, the doctor said, but she'll hurt a lot, for a while.* We don't have to walk if you don't want to. Maybe later? No, no, I'm not leaving. I'll stay right here, ta bien? Your Mami's making her famous Rice with Coconut, and your Papi's coming home early from work. No, don't cry, Paolita. I'm not leaving. *And she did. She cried from the pain. More, more painkillers, please, she begged. She was going to die, she was sure. Nothing had ever hurt so much. Like, she told her sons, like a hand is pulling your insides out, all of you, pulling it out. Please, I need pills, or shots, or whatever they give you. I can't stand it. Please! She cried.* You like your stuffed animalito? Look at his eyes, aren't they funny? What is it, anyway, is it an elephant? Yes! I think it's an elephant, look at his ears and his trompa. *He and his father stayed with her the entire time she was in the clinic. They would take turns sleeping, watching, and keeping her company.* I'm coming back. And we'll go to the park. But you have to get better, soon, all right? You promise? That's my girl!

Dear Nito,

How are ya Big Bro? I'm doing fine over here, behaving and having a good time and reading and studying hard. Did I ever tell you about Louis? I think I did, way back before I was in the 8th grade, no? He gave me a record of QUIET STRIKE. I think I'm in love! Papi and Mami don't know this, of course. They think Louis and me are just friends. But we're more than friends. I'm glad that Papi likes him. I think he likes him because Louis is Cuban just like us. You know, the patria thing, Papi's big into that. I don't mind. I like to hear stories about Cuba and I love the food that Mami cooks, all Cuban. I don't like the coffee, though. Never liked it and never will. I do like the music, Salsa and the more mellow stuff like the music you did in Spain. Anyway, I was telling you about Louis. He says when he finishes school he wants to join the Air Force. I tell him fine, as long as you write to me and we keep in touch.

How do I know I'm in love with him? Well, you should know, you're in love with Erica, aren't you? You've been with her for months now. How long? I like Erica a lot. She's different. I like people that are different. Tell her I send her a big elephant kiss and an O-S-O hug. I know I'm in love with Louis because I think about him every day. And I like to be with him. We break together. He's a great breaker! I also like it when he kisses me (on the cheek, don't get ideas!). Sometimes Mami takes us to the movies. Louis likes the ones with action, like all the Star War movies and The Temple of Doom and other ones that I can't remember. Louis and I talk about staying together for the rest of our lives. We dream about our home and our children. But we don't do anything bad, I promise you. We just sit there and listen to good rapping music and daydream. By the way, is your band going to do some rapping stuff some day? I can rap real well, you know.

Well, Big Bro, I'm glad that I can tell you all these things. You are the only person in this big wide world that understands me completely and who I can tell every one of my feelings. I love you so much, Nito.

IN-LOVE,

Geneia

When All Is *Quiet* And It Rains

In the evenings, especially when it rained, she missed Lucie and Passa. The way they ran after each other, like Andre and Paola. The way Lucie licked Passa's face and paws, the way Passa kneaded Lucie's belly, the way they watched each other sleep. She missed most of all the way Raúl talked to the animals. Mussu Mussu, he called the cat. Negrita was the name he gave the dog. He would take a thread and tickle Passa's nose when she was sleeping. He was rough with Lucie. He would push her and pinch her pink tongue and he would tie a rope around her tail and make her go crazy, around and around, trying to get rid of it. Raúl loved to see her doing that. You could hear his laughter all the way out to the street. Lucie and Passa, those two negras are something else, he'd say once in a while, like he was talking about people.

She resented the fact that her children always dumped all their unwanted things in her apartment. Furniture, boxes full of records, Juan's paints and brushes. Junk. And those animals. She had hated animals as long as she could remember. Gladys wanted to have a pet. Not in the house she couldn't. If her daughter wanted to feed the neighborhood cats, that was okay. But no pets in the house. She'd had her share of animals when she was a young girl. She fought with Juan when he brought her Lucie. "Take that ugly dog out of here!" But Juan said no. That was his mother Josefa's pet and his landlord didn't want pets. So she had to keep it. That was that.

Juan and Gladys eventually moved to a house with a huge back yard and they bought a German shephard, Princesa. Horrible animal. Pushy and hurtful. The stupid dog had the habit of jumping all over you and licking your face. That tongue! That slimy tongue! How could Americans let dogs kiss their faces like that? How could they? Dogs had germs and bacteria and their breath stunk. Americans were crazy,

135

for that and many other reasons. And Juan never took Lucie back, even after they moved to the house. By now, Raúl had gotten attached to the animalito, and as hard as it was for her to admit it, so had she. Then one day, Nito showed up with a box in his hands. He opened it and there she found his black cat, Passa. Her grandson was going on a long trip so could she please take care of it for a while, maybe keep her for good? Her mouth dropped open. Didn't she have enough already with Josefa's dog? And a black cat to top it all off! Black like the night.

She complained to him about the work, about Raúl's unwillingness to help around the house, to do the shopping, the laundry. "Raúl," she told her grandson, "believes that a man's work is outside the house. But there isn't anything for him to do out there. He waters the plants and sweeps the driveway, and once a week he takes out the tenants' trash, but other than that, what is there for him to do outside the house?" It was inside where things needed to be done. Maybe not cooking, he didn't know how to do that, but washing the dishes, vacuuming the carpet, cleaning the bathroom, doing the laundry. There was so much he could do to help her. Her grandson brought from the trunk of his car a plastic box and two gigantic bags of dirt. "In the box," he said, "Passa does her thing. You have to fill it up with this sand. And then, sorry Abuela, then you have to pick up her turds with this spoon." She just about fainted. Why did all her children feel they had the right to make these demands on her? Why?

When Lucie started scratching her back they took her to the doctor. There was a hospital for animals where they operated on them and gave them injections and pills, just like humans. Unbelievable, she thought. The doctor prescribed some cream and it worked for a while. But Lucie went back to her desperate scratching. She began to lose her hair and her skin showed, raw and smelly. They took her back to the hospital and this time they kept her there for days. When they brought her home her skin had healed and some of her black fluffy hair had returned. But now she seemed tired and lazy. She hardly played with Passa. She slept all the time and dragged her paws around like they weighed a ton. The dog had gotten old, very old.

They live fourteen, fifteen years at the most, she thought. Then one day, all of a sudden, they age, they begin to look tired, a cloud appears in their eyes and the hair around their noses turns white. They don't run to you when you call them. They don't jump up when you get home. They just look tired. She was told from a very early age that one shouldn't cry over the death of animals. But she couldn't stop the tears when she found Lucie one morning, sleeping peacefully, the cat resting her head on the dog's belly. She didn't have to touch Lucie nor try to wake her up to know that she was dead. She picked up the body and held it to her bosom. She held it there and kissed it. She kissed it! She couldn't help herself. And the warm skin of her dog didn't feel dirty and it didn't smell bad. Passa knew her friend had died. She pressed against Eusebia's legs, she looked up, she meowed, she cried. Then Eusebia put Lucie down on the couch and Passa jumped up and licked the dog all over, on her belly, on her ears, on her mouth. "No use, Passa. You can't make her better. You can't bring her back. But she knows you loved her. And she knows how sad you are."

They told her that Passa died from food poisoning. Hah! Food poisoning, sure. How could she die from that. She was fed the best food, the one they advertised on American television. Passa couldn't have died from that. She knew why she'd died. She missed Lucie. Poor Passa. She didn't go quietly and peacefully the way Lucie did. She started vomiting this green stuff and she got skinny and ugly and lost all her vigor. Her fur was no longer silky and shiny. She would spend the day pacing up and down the apartment, sniffing everything like a dog, looking for her friend. Then she had convulsions.

That's when they took her away. And she never returned.

Lucie and Passa. Those two negras are something else, he'd say once in a while, like he was talking about people . . .

Dear Julian,

Guess what? I got my period! It hurts and Mami went to get me some of those pads, like the ones she uses but smaller. It was about time, Abuela says. Why, she started having her menstruation when she was ten!

When it started I got real nervous and scared. I had no idea what was going on. Mami hadn't told me what would happen when it came. She just said, Genny, one of these days you're going to notice some blood in your panties and when that happens you'll be a woman, not a kid anymore. Whoopee, I said, I can't wait to be a woman! But now, to tell you the honest truth, I just think it's a big pain, in every sense of the word. You have to keep that bulky thing down there and worry about the stains and put up with the cramps and I tell you, Bro, you're lucky you're a man.

I was over at Johnny and Laura's, when they were having this big party for the family. That's when it happened. I wish you'd been there. It would've been easier. I was surrounded by all those Colombians and Mami was busy helping Laura in the kitchen and Laura's mom, Mariana, you know how loud she talks, and Abuela was just sitting there pretending to listen. She doesn't like Mariana. She says that all of Laura's relatives think they're very important, because some of them are doctors and lawyers and they have maids over there in Bogotá. Well, Mariana was going on and on about all her exhibitions and her latest collection and the wonderful reviews she got in Los Angeles and how famous she is and how she's the only Colombian artist who's respected and admired outside Colombia. And there I was, feeling like crap, with this queasy feeling in my stomach and a tickling down there, between my legs, and a sharp pain and a funny sensation like I was peeing in my pants, but it didn't feel like peeing, it was more like after you pee and you feel all wet and yucky.

That night Mami talked to me for a long time and told me about sex and children and you know. Nothing new to me. She was so nervous, pobrecita, she could hardly get her words out. I sat quietly and listened, pretending to be learning from her.

I hope Erica comes with you next time you visit. I have a lot of questions to ask her about this mess I'm in. Tell her I say hi. And thank you for being the best Bro in the whole world.

WOMAN

Geneia

The Master Plan

One day I decided to leave my house in West Los Angeles and get an apartment in the same building where my family lives, on the corner of 135th Street and Hawthorne Boulevard. Erica's master plan had led to this: a platinum album; a contract for two more l.p.'s; offers for TV appearances; opening for MIAMI SOUNDS and later touring, as the main band, all of the United States, Latin America and Japan. My grandfather was dying, so I had the perfect excuse to escape all the sudden attention. This time I *really* needed to be near the family. After Abuelo's death, my grandmother asked me if I could please take care of her, so I let her move in with me. The perfect arrangement: All she had to do now to reach her daughter was to walk a few feet. Eventually, I warned her, I would have to go back to my piano and my home in West Los Angeles. I would continue, however, to pay her rent and tend to her needs. She agreed. She wanted me there, keeping her company, for just a few more days . . .

"Dios mío! What am I going to do?! The phone won't work!" She fiddled with the machine and hit it repeatedly. "Do something, Nito!" The phone started working again. "Thank you, Lord!"

Was Gladys supposed to go to the dentist today or tomorrow? Was it today? Is that why she's so late? (Ten minutes late.) What if her daughter was alone, stranded, her car broken down, in the middle of nowhere? What if she's getting mugged this very second? What if?!! What if?!! His grandmother had him call the ITC. No luck. She called several of the people Gladys worked with. No, they didn't know where she was. Gladys finally "checked in." Thank God and all the saints. Thank the Virgen del Cobre, thank the Lord her daughter was fine and on her way home. She had stopped over at a friend's house to pick up some Avon products. How could she, Eusebia shouted over the phone, how could she do this to her? (Do what, Abuela? Do what?!) Was it fair? And now, oh no, now she would be caught in traffic, during rush hour!

Why, he asked her, realizing much too well the futility of the question. Why are you this way, Abuela? Why do you worry so much about us? (She demanded to be told every move and every plan. And she contested every decision. Nothing could be done that she didn't object to, from the very minor details to the major ones: shopping, driving, taking a shit in public restrooms.) *I want to know, I need to know, I have to know, I deserve to know.* But why? First, she would say, because I love you all so much and loving is worrying. Second, because Gladys is careless and absent-minded, she loses things and drives too fast and . . . (she's dumb, right, Abuela?) And third, because I was born this way and I can't change. (But didn't you used to say that even lions, the most fierce and savage of animals, even they could be tamed and made to change? Didn't you say that when talking about Papi?) Besides, how could we expect her to be calm when she had been taking care of a dying man during the last three years? The situation affected her. Coudn't we see it? She hadn't always been this nervous and fearful. (Of course!)

I'm so happy that you're here, Nito. It makes everything easier.

Not for me.

It's good for you to be here, resting, eating well . . . If only you didn't have to write so much . . . What are you writing, muchachito, letters to your girlfriends?

Yes, Abuela, letters to my girlfriends.

And when are you gonna get married, eh? Give me a

chance to see your Julianitos before I die?

Enjoy Johnny's kids and leave me alone, Abuela.

Why do you talk to me that way? Don't you love me?

Sometimes it's difficult to love you, Abuela.

Why?

Because you won't give us room to breathe.

Can I help it if I have so much love to give?

I don't want that much love.

Don't be so ungrateful, mijo.

I'm going to lock you up if you continue to bug us all so much.

Ah, now you're joking, jaraneando, right? Tell me you were joking, mijo, when you said that.

I was dead serious.

You've forgotten the sacrifices I made for you.

No, Abuela, I haven't forgotten them, but.

The times I ran to your bedside when you were ill. It was me you called when you felt frightened.

But I'm not frightened anymore.

You should be.

Yes, living is dangerous, so?

There are dangers one can avoid.

Breathing, for example? . . . Why am I here listening to you?!

Because I'm wiser than you, even if you think I'm a vieja loca. Some day you'll realize it. Some day, when I'm gone, you'll think of me and realize just how right I was.

I was experiencing insanity (*her* insanity) as never before. It all seemed like a telenovela (one of the many she watched thanks to SIB) and I was playing the villain! The moment I remotely suspected an oncoming argument, or heard Papi utter an unfair remark or raise his voice, I would start screaming like a madman, hit the wall, slam the door, chain smoke as I drove down Hawthorne Boulevard, blaming him (them) for my unhappiness and suffering. Like a child, brooding, restless, impotent.

When I refused to see a shrink (convinced that I wasn't the one, or the only one needing professional help in my family), Laura suggested that I put down my experiences on paper or tape. She said it would help sort through things, clear out the bad feelings. Write it all as if you were telling a story to someone, she said, to my sister, to Erica, or to myself. She gave me books, many by her famous compatriot, García Márquez, and other ones by writers of something she calls the "Latin American Boom." What a ridiculous name, I thought. I read *One Hundred Years of Solitude* and found it fascinating. Will our wheel of madness, I asked myself, like the Buendias' wheel of solitude, stop turning some day? Will there be a rupture, an end to it all?

I started to jot down conversations I had heard at home. For some reason (to save time?) I wrote them all down in English, as if they had already been translated into that language in my head. I transcribed old family recordings, rescued notes I had taken through the years and pages from my diaries. I tried to probe into my grandfather's madness, and I appropriated twenty of my sister's letters. I made an effort not to see things only through my eyes and not to write a straightforward biography, which is precisely what Novel Records wanted me to do once I told them I was writing a book. (One more American Success Story!!) My objective became clear in a very early stage of the writing process: I was to become one more character, deserving of the right to my own type of insanity . . .

He took a long walk along the beach and then plunged into the surf, hoping the cold water would wake him up from the horror of death. His grandfather was gone, and had left slowly and painfully, the way he had hoped it wouldn't happen. He sat on the sand, the waves bathing his feet. The beach was deserted this early in the morning. A few hours alone to think or just to be. So easy to jump in and fuse oneself with the deep blues and greens. The beach (Manhattan, Hermosa, Redondo) always had the same effect on him. It made everything outside of it seem small and trivial. It also brought out the worst cliches. Was it possible to write songs about the California beaches anymore? Poetry, perhaps? Trite, empty verses. But triteness and emptiness were the main requisites of popular music in the eighties. Americans wanted to be *entertained*. Record-buying Americans especially. The ones who made him a "star." Julian Toledo, the up-and-coming Hispanic rocker, image of the Crossover Dream, was just another entertainer . . . *JULIAN AND THE L.A. SCENE's debut album, Once Upon a Time in the City of Angels, is a serious production. Their music is an effortless flow of acoustic, jazzy sounds that blend the best of American White Pop and Ethnic Rock. However, they don't have the bombastic repetitive sonic aggression of the more militant Salsa enfants terribles. Julian runs smoothly down his own path, providing the listener with subtle and impressionistic melodies like that of "Spring," and sentimental pieces like "Tropical Nights (I Hear Voices)," that evoke nostalgia and reminiscence . . .*

A luxurious mansion on Wilshire Boulevard, West Los Angeles, in the heart of "the business," relatively close to Hawthorne but far, so far from his little Cuban family, far from the Island they had recreated in suburban L.A. In his world no trace of the past could be found. Sparse but comfortable furniture. State of the art sound equipment. Never the smell of fried plantain nor the boisterous parental laughter. An answering machine that protected him from his grandmother. Lots of foliage and a hammock hung between oak trees in the backyard. A weeping willow, a picnic table. A swimming pool and the most common of American signs: a barbecue grill. The caressing silence broken by his piano playing. Broken, at times, in the evenings, by the band's rehearsals, or by his love-making. Loud love he made to Erica. Erica who liked to run naked through the semi-empty rooms, the whiteness of her skin blending with that of the barren walls. Loud love he made to Erica-the-Shadow and that never lasted long enough, that always left him drained and peaceful. Had his parents known this kind of love? Had his grandmother? Will his sister? . . . *Julian's piano solos are masterful and sensitively woven, but it's mostly Erica Johnson's melodic vision that sees the album through. Her voice burnished to a warm, grainy rasp, she breezes through the lyrics in total control. It is ultimately Erica Johnson that makes Once Upon a Time in the City of Angels a winner by any standard . . .*

Fighting the waves. A useful metaphor. Useful for what? Who cared about his life-long battle? Another struggling artist in search of home. Against the odds. Thrown into the vastness of a foreign and threatening ocean. Unable to swim (Remember, Abuela, when I asked to be given swimming lessons, back in the days of Varadero, and you raised hell? Swimming was dangerous. Why, you could drown!) It was strange. Like gravity. Stronger than his will to be free. They called and he ran to their feet. The familial summoning was heard more powerful than ever before. The recorded message bounced off the walls and pierced his brain, pecking at it like a famished bird of prey over its victim. His father: "Come home immediately!" His grandmother: "Please, mijo, come home . . ." His mother: "Home . . . home . . . home immediately!" When did it start, this madness? Long before he was born, no doubt. Long before any member of his family existed. The Island. Spain. Africa. Who could trace it all the way back, and for what purpose?

He had indeed come home *immediately* in order to become a faithful and abiding member of the clan. Don't resist the pull of history, Julian Toledo. Give up the treasured American realm of individuality. No room for individuals in your culture. No such thing as a floating self . . . *It's the rage now for Pop bands to put a little Latin in their tracks, or to sprinkle their lyrics with some Spanish. But most of them see ethnic as nothing more than musical dress-up. By contrast, JULIAN AND THE L.A. SCENE takes a real and believable Latin Approach to pop rock. The band de-emphasizes the mannerisms that have marked so many recent groups. Its members use some traditional musical formulas, but their lyrics are forceful and socially charged: "The lights of the Bronx still shine/ but Liberty's gone and people die/ It happened once upon a time/ said Picasso . . ."*

Julian Toledo would never be anything but a renegade Cuban. Cubano resentido, as his father self-righteously said: resentful of his culture, snobbish, believing himself to be better, or "different." The bottom line is, Julianito, that you were not even born in the United States . . . *If you look at the top ten selling songs today you will find that half, if not more, of the hits listed are refried and resurrected oldies. The energy and rage of the Breaking and Rapping ghetto artists have entered the mainstream and become silent. Breakers have been given a piece of the dream. They are now part of an American institution. What has become of New Wave? Well, it's no longer "new", but it can still be considered a "wave", a wave of repetition and rehashing . . .* Is that what he wished so desperately for? To be a "true" American? What did that imply? No, it was rather a matter of always having to remember and return to the pain, having to face it over and over again . . . *The labels have changed. One doesn't speak of disco, even if a lot of the music being done today sounds like that discredited American genre. One talks of "danceables," "good beats," "driving rhythms," "happening tracks," "current attractions," terms which have all been used to describe JULIAN AND THE L.A. SCENE's de-*

but album, Once Upon a Time in the City of Angels, . . . Did his music tell a story? If someone were to read, really read his words, would they be able to hear him? *. . . This recently formed group claims to have a message. Lead singer Erica Johnson has stated that their songs "deal with important issues." Perhaps they do. But in order to get at the root of these issues, the listener has to put up with embellished, tedious, artificial, studio-fabricated Latin sounds that owe more to Lionel Richie's "All Night Long (All Night)" than to any Caribbean island influence . . .* Words didn't matter anymore. No one read them *. . . Once Upon a Time in the City of Angels has been described by respectable critics as one of the best American record productions of the year. After such claims, I was naturally a little skeptical when I listened to Julian and his Angelenos . . .* He was asked to "trim down" the lyrics and use more catchy refrains. Lots of danceable junk, the company said, and as few verses as possible *. . . I found the record at first entertaining, progressively depressing, but more than anything suddenly a bore. Their lyrics that speak against militarism and the commercialization of art fall flat when delivered through bombastic, heavily orchestrated arrangements that make Bonnie Tyler's "Total Eclipse of the Heart" sound a capella . . .* Surrounded by Erica, Roli, Joe, Lucho and five Novel gangsters, he had stamped his signature on a thousand papers *. . . Once Upon a Time wants to appeal to a wide array of listeners and at the same time make strong statements. What it attains through its ambitious eclecticism is a very confused and annoying concoction, one that fails to raise this listener's consciousness and instead bores him to tears . . .*

If only the voices would stop. A horrible and tempting thought. The most gruesome of crimes. The thought was there gleaming under the sun, splashing on the shore like a wave, possessing him like a demon. It was comforting and conciliatory the way some dreams are. Destroy the source of pain. Break away, once and for all, with the Last of the Mambisas. Walk quietly (she's a light sleeper) into her room and put a pillow over her head, and hold it there, tight, for a few minutes . . . Just a few minutes . . . There, so easy. The town would read the next day another one of its not unusual stories: HISPANIC MUSICIAN KILLS GRANDMOTHER. And in fine print: He could no longer bear to hear her squeaking voice, or accept the kisses from her lipless, slobbering mouth. He could no longer bear to see, in dreams as in reality, her wide open eyes, terrified, afraid of life. L.A. SCENE and Novel Records would rejoice in the publicity. He would be locked up to rot forever (saved from the death penalty by reason of insanity), but his albums would sell. She was a saint. She had no life of her own. She lived and died for her family. Ungrateful bastard. Son of the devil. May he burn eternally in hell! No, he could never, would never do it. But the thought gleamed under the sun, splashing its whiteness on the shore, coming back to bathe him for as long as he endured the coldness of the water, for as long as he held it the way he held and crushed a tiny crab in his hands, for as long as the sun would shine, it persisted.

The interview took place in the Hawthorne apartment, a few days after the death of Abuelo. I'm still not sure why I agreed to do it just then. All the other members of L.A. SCENE, including Erica, had been blabbering all over the place to the media. I had resisted the temptation. I had refused to be quoted, to be asked questions by people who wanted to produce nothing but their own versions of my success. Why give the interview now, I asked myself. Was I seeking to satisfy a need for martyrdom, appearing humble and unmarred by my sudden fame, devoted to my family, made into a symbol of strong cultural roots? Now, I thought, when I finally swim in the Mainstream, I am opening the doors of an apartment where I live with my grandmother, where I spend hours consoling her and the other members of the family, listening to their soap opera preoccupations. Nothing here smells of America. Nothing points to the fact that I have "made it." Erica, I later told the *Rocks* interviewer, doesn't understand why I'm so attached to my folks. But hell, I'll say it again, I can't just all of a sudden turn around and claim to be an orphan. It's just not that simple. In any case, the band is rehearsing again (for our quote unquote second l.p.) and I have been contacted by a publisher who's interested in reading my "biography." I have continued working as musical director for the group, although most of the songs and arrangements are being written by Erica. None of the guys welcomed my idea of changing our name to ERICA AND L.A. SCENE. I assured them, and so did Erica, that the contracts would remain, monetarily speaking, intact. All the group members would be given credit for their contributions to future albums as they were in *Once Upon a Time*. The new name was a gimmick, as reps from Novel Records were glad to point out, and they supported my suggestion wholeheartedly.

Julian Toledo is tall and muscular. His handsome Latin face, reminiscent of the Hollywood silent movies, seems to show a lack of sleep. When he speaks, a slight Spanish accent comes out now and then, mainly noticeable in the strange idiomatic licenses (all of which were deleted for publication, of course) that the singer-songwriter takes with the English language. He is wearing (the ever-present) brown-tinted sunglasses, a sleeveless white T-shirt, black vest, black jeans. He puffs hard on a Golden Light, his head bobbing rhythmically to the colossal Latin shuffle that is thundering from the speakers above his head. The guitars crackle, the horns honk and wail, the drums rumble wildly. The room returns to silence. Then "Tropical Nights" comes on: "Tropical Nights/I hear voices/Anger and tears/I hear voices . . ." Julian intimates that he's ready to answer my questions.

You've been described as a newcomer to the American music scene, but your band has been around since the seventies . . .

Our music goes back a long time, yes, long before Erica came into the picture. We did our first album in Spain, in '77.

Was the record a hit?

No, not really.

What kind of material went into your second album?

I wanted to make music for the Hispanic people of the United States, so I started writing songs like "Family Portrait," that dealt with themes of exile, alienation, language barriers, cultural stereotypes.

Was this second record more successful?

No. Young Hispanic Americans didn't buy our message. They didn't "relate." The older folks, the ones we thought would understand us, they had to face the problems of exile every day; they didn't want to be reminded. If we were to reach them, we were gonna have to sound more commercial, you know, meaningless lyrics, catchy melodies, big orchestras, female choruses that go la la la at all the right moments. We couldn't do that stuff. That's more or less what we'd done the first time around. That wasn't us. So our second album sat in the record stores collecting dust. Once in a while we'd hear one of our songs on the Hispanic stations in L.A.

How did you survive through all that? Financially, I mean.

We'd do a lot of clubs and parties. That kept us going.

Have you read the reviews of your platinum album?

Yes. They either say we're the best thing to come along since Ricky Ricardo or they give us the "lot of hype about nothing" routine. Some reviewers talk about us as if we were part of some frustrated and failed revolution. They all seem to like Erica.

Does that bother you?

No. She's had a lot to do with the way we sound today. Erica's a great singer.

How do you feel about all the attention that your band is getting?

We see these labels all over the place, you know, "Caribbean Pop Rock," "The Revival," "The Latin Scene in the US." "Julian and the Soulful Angelenos." (We hear stories about Erica, how she went around offering herself to the old boys in Hollywood to get signed and produced.) One day we're barely making it, the next day our music is being played by all the major rock and pop stations in the country. We walk into a dance club in West L.A. and there is "City of Angels," blasting out, our rhythms bursting out as the sweat runs down the young bodies of the eighties. (Slick, beautiful) teenagers moving their shoulders (and their hips) like Charo and Rita Moreno. "Latin's hot, man!" "It's happening!" "That sound is raging!" "Maximum raging!"

Are you planning to do another album in Spanish?

Well, now, because we've made it in the American market, the Spanish record companies are begging us to record with them. SIB (Spanish International Broadcasting, those gangsters), they're calling us every day and offering us money, (lots of money) if we agree to appear on their talk shows like "Hispanidad." They can beg until they're blue in the face.

But obviously not everyone in your band feels the way you do . . .

The guys are getting blown away by all the attention, especially Joe. (He's been blabbing all this shit about how we suffered and how we've had a long via cruxis and how we deserve to get a piece of the pie after all those sacrifices.) But one good thing has come out of all the publicity: the young kids, second and third generation Cubans, Mexicans, Puerto Ricans, they're listening to us now. My sister, you know, she keeps me up on what the young ones are saying; she's like my eyes and ears in that age group.

And what are the young listeners saying?

They talk about our music and they like the fact that we're Cuban Americans. Now, there's a certain pride in being Hispanic-American, you know, in knowing Spanish. (Now, who's that pop female singer who started the whole ball rolling? The one who made Spanish the in, avant-garde language for popular American music?)

How did you and Erica meet?

We met at a party in Hollywood.

Did she like your band, at first . . . ?

She said, "Look, your music's good, but you can't sit around and expect people to buy it just because it's honest and from the heart." She laid out a plan. Step one, she said, make a tape and give it to Mark Davis of The Animals. She knew him well and she thought that Mark could at least give us some advice. For the demo we did "Crazy Love," the Paul Anka song from the early sixties which now has become part of "The Revival."

Does the song mean anything special to you? Is there a story behind it?

When people hear "Crazy Love," they immediately think it's about a love affair, a cursed romance. And that's in the song, sure, "Everything's wrong/Heaven above/Set me free/ From this crazy love . . ." But for me the song is also about the love of music, about relationships . . . , about family . . .

About family?!!

About relationships in general . . .

Is anybody else in your family musically oriented?

My brother used to play the drums (I have no problems with Johnny, as long as we don't talk about certain things . . .); my sister is good at writing poetry. She also writes great letters.

Let's go back to "The Plan." Did Davis like your demo of "Crazy Love"?

He liked it. He passed it on to Carl Stein, an engineer at The Animals' Syncro Sound studio in Hollywood. Stein had all the contacts. If we could work with him, we'd have a chance.

So Erica Johnson was your liaison.

She connected us with Davis, who connected us with Stein, who introduced us to the person who would eventually become our producer, John Carroll. And there wasn't a single detail that she didn't plan . . . She didn't want us to look too trendy. Our image was classy and Latin, according to her. Not as impeccable as Roli's, but classy. She looked at my songs, picked five or six, learned them, wrote three new melodies and came back with more ideas . . .

Step Two?

Yes. Our music was to match the bleak lyrics that reflected my personal "protests." Words and music woven together with subdued post-punk guitar and synthesizer licks. Cymbals and brass for a couple of upbeat Latin numbers. The whole country was into nostalgia, so if I wanted to, Erica said, I could do a couple of oldies. Songs from my childhood on the poor side of a Cuban town, songs from a jukebox that burst with boleros and rock and roll ballads, "Diana," "Put Your Head on My Shoulder," "Oh Carol." American songs that no one in the barrio understood, but that everybody mimicked and hummed: "Be My Baby," "Will You Still Love Me Tomorrow?," "Adam and Eve," "Crazy Love."

Was there a third step?

Yes: Novel Records. The supposedly new band, with Erica singing most of the vocals, hadn't been together five months when our second demo, "Once Upon a Time (In the City of Angels)" had already gone into heavy rotation. Less than a year later, JULIAN AND THE L.A. SCENE was signing with Novel Records.

How did Novel see you, potentially, that is?

As a true winner. (We had already done two albums, two records that sold badly but that made us a familiar name in the predominantly Hispanic communities in the US and also in Spain and Mexico. There was to be no mention of those records. They didn't exist. We were told by Novel right off that in order for the group to make it in America, and before they would sign us, we were to forget what we'd done up until now. None of that would help, they said. It's all in the past, a small past, they insisted, and now we were thinking big, big like this great country.)

What attracted you to Erica?

I liked her locura, her madness you know. Erica's been

breaking rules all her life. No one believes that she grew up in Yoder, a small town in Kansas, that her parents are Mennonites.

How does Erica feel about your strong family ties?

She doesn't understand the attachment. (She hates my father and she thinks my grandmother is a demented woman who should be locked up.) But I can't just all of a sudden turn around and say forget you all, I'm an orphan. It's different with us. We're Cubanos.

Obviously, Erica's "Master Plan" is working.

Obviously . . .

You have contributed to "The Revival" with your remakes of Paul Anka's early songs, "Crazy Love," "Put Your Head on My Shoulder," and also with your own material, which has a certain mood and echo of the forties and fifties. How do you feel about this return to the past, which is not just in music but also in fashion and, you might say, in the way of thinking of the American people?

It's interesting that mainly the forties and fifties are back. The forties, you know, the baggy pants. The fifties, the blue jeans with the button-down shirts and, you know, the argyle sweaters. Those fashions are from a very pure and conservative era. Vacation Land USA. Not a care in the world. Everybody owned a house with a picket fence. You had your occasional rebels who followed the James Dean model, but it's basically the Leave It To Beaver lifestyle, in contrast to the sixties and the early seventies during Viet Nam when families were in an uproar.

Do you like living in the United States?

I like the "American Concept." But the average American is very ignorant of what actually goes on behind closed doors. And there's nothing we can do. We have no power.

But don't you think that a musician, more than any other artist, can have a tremendous impact on the masses?

What can my music do in the face of nuclear armament? Or against the Department of Defense of this country? They let me play and sing and get rich as long as I don't threaten their status in any real way. If I had any potential to affect it, I assure you, I wouldn't be so free to speak my mind or to make music.

If you played in Cuba, for example?

Yes.

Will you do it?

I don't know.)

How do you feel about your success?

It doesn't seem real yet.

TROPICAL NIGHTS (I HEAR VOICES)

(Lyrics by Julian Toledo; Music by Erica Johnson)

There was a kiosk at the corner.
They sold sugar cane drinks and
overflowing black bean soup.
An old jukebox sang songs
of broken hearts and neverending blues.

There was a woman
who prayed to her saints
day and night.
I remember her voice.
It still rings in my ears,
full of anger and tears.
I've been hearing her voice
all my life.

There was a boy
who believed in his grandmother's dreams.
Sleep only came when he felt her embrace,
when she whispered to him
songs of mythical birds
in the tropical nights.

I remember the voices.
They come back now and then.
In the warm days of summer,
the voices.
I still hear their refrain.

ONCE UPON A TIME (IN THE CITY OF ANGELS)

(Lyrics and music by Julian Toledo)

When you're here
you will forget where you came from
You can be just who you want to be
The time is right
if you can fly with the angels
Just don't look back
the past is past
you're a star

Now you're a star
You're part of us
Angels
Now you're a star
You're part of us
You're in the City of Lights

When you're here you play the game
if you wanna be high
Hear the beat and let yourself
be taken up in flight
You'll have to find
your way some day
like the angels
You'll have to find
your way some day
to the lights

Now hear the beat
You're flying high
Angels
Now hear the beat

You're flying high
You're in the City of Lights

Just don't look back
the past is past
you're in the city of angels
Cause you're a star
you're part of us
you're in the city of lights
Once upon a time in the city of lights
Once upon a time there were angels
Angels . . .
Angels . . .

SPRING

(Lyrics and music by Julian Toledo)

It's bright outside
and I'm a silhouette.
It's peaceful now
and I have no regrets.
Not because of the spring
that suddenly arrives.
Not because of this need
to be sharing my life,
A distant time of dreams,
of fears that never died,
hands full of love
that couldn't be
discarded.

I never thought
I'd be a silhouette
or that I'd feel the warmth
of your caress.
I never thought
one could sing of the spring
joyfully,
lovingly
again.

It's bright outside
and I'm a silhouette.
I look at you.
I can't accept it yet.
I'm going now, my friend,

a fading silly silhouette.

It's bright outside
and I have no regrets.

GUERNICA IN NEW YORK

(Lyrics by Julian Toledo; Music by Erica Johnson)

We shall speak
of spermcut styles
under the heat
of a neon sign
A place to hide
where suddenly the air is cool
and New York is a tour
of thirsty T-shirt buyers

Numb city looks
anticipating the war goddess
the horrible seductive
Guernica
We will have to sing her song
in the name of her Father
the Sun
and Picasso

We will remember
the sweat along our backs
the sound in countertime
of Apple boxes
the lights of the Bronx still shine
but Liberty's gone and people die
It happened once upon a time
said Picasso

And we will again
feel the breeze that erases
the smell of this place
that's pressed in our skin

as we run down the walkway
another door
another home without a key
without a lock
where people starve
He could've said it so
I'm sure
Oh sure
He would've said too
Picasso

We shall finally see
a button off Broadway
I LOVE NEW YORK NEW YORK
I love New York you know
the way I love
my Florsheim shoes
my Gucci bag
my Vidal mousse
I love New York New York you know
the way I love you GUERNICA
painted once more
the way he did it then,
painted again
and again and again
by Picasso

J.T.
July 14, 1987

164

Dear Nito,

I hope this letter gets to you before Papi's. I have to warn you about a lot of things he's going to say to you. First of all, he wants you to finish out all your contracts and don't sign any more and don't get involved with that record company that wants to make you into a star. None of that. No more. Because he's going to give you three weeks, he says, to get out of all your commitments and move back to Hawthorne. Papi says you could play your music here if you wanted to, in town, close to us.

He says he's not going to ask you all this as a favor, no, he says he's going to demand it of you, because it is your duty and your responsibility to be with the family at a time of trouble. I thought I'd warn you so you'd have time to think about what to tell him. I would love for you to move back to Hawthorne, Nito, you know that. Nothing would make me happier, but to tell you the truth, I think it's unfair to make those demands on you, as if you didn't have your own life to live and your home with Erica and your career. Papi is going to talk to you about Erica too. He has been discussing her with Abuela a lot lately. They sit in the kitchen, in her apartment, after they clean up Abuelo, and they talk about you while they drink coffee. If Mami's there she does her usual thing, she sits and listens, never says a word. Do you ever wonder what she thinks and how she feels? I love my Mami.

And what do they say? Well, they say that your "arrangement" with Erica is a bad example for me, that that is no way to carry on in life. Erica's a bad influence, because she doesn't look "normal." They say that they love you, especially Abuela, but that you have let them down time after time. First, by studying music at school. Papi wanted you to be in business, right? Then you let them down by moving all the time, moving far from us. Even if you're just in West

L.A. you're still far, they say. Johnny got married and has a family, they claim, and he didn't move away, well, just a couple of cities down from Hawthorne. Then you let them down by dressing like a hippie, with long hair and torn up blue jeans, with all those necklaces you wore like a woman and you walked around barefoot all the time. Weren't you just a kid in the sixties, though? I guess you were a very young hippie. Papi says that he nearly died of embarrassment when you arrived at the house and the neighbors (the Cuban neighbors!) saw you. And then you let them down when you decided to form your band and you got an agent and that damned agent sent you to play in corrupted places. And you would come home looking like you hadn't eaten in days, because you spent so much time rehearsing your numbers and not making a penny. Then, they say, you let them down by having a relationship with Erica. She looks like she takes drugs, they say. How could you let a gringa like that be your companion, they ask, a woman who doesn't even know how to cook a decent meal. Abuela says that before she dies, she wants to see your children, you have to give her that pleasure before she dies, she tells Papi. And get married before that, of course.

Abuelo's getting worse all the time. He doesn't talk and he can't move and they have to do everything for him. He sits there the entire day, except for when Papi unties him and forces him to walk. There's nothing you could do to make things better, Nito, but according to Abuela they need you, and they need you close by, in the neighborhood or in the same apartment building. And you have to give up your life and your girlfriend and your music. That's not fair. Now that things are finally happening. When you're almost a star. So I thought I'd warn you.

You always say that you love me more than anybody in this world. Well, Big Bro, I feel the same way about you. I look forward to seeing you again. And Erica! But don't move down here just because Abuelo's ill. There's nothing you or anyone can do to help him now. Tell Papi you'll come for a few days, but don't give up your concerts and your contract with that big record company. Don't give up your life. It's so unfair!

YOUR BIGGEST FAN

Geneia